BLUES DANCE

a novel by

Amon Saba Saakana

BLUES DANCE

a novel by Amon Saba Saakana

First edition published in Britain 1985

Karnak House,
300 Westbourne Park Road,
London W11 1EH

ISBN 0 907015 14 X hardback
ISBN 0 907015 15 8 paperback

For Gem & Shabaka & Kashta
Dennis Bovell
& members of Brimstone:
Gus, Leo, Sam, Vivienne, Eyes, Bassie, Scruff

Sir Coxsone . . . Duke Reid . . . Jah Sufferer . . . Neville the Enchanter . . . Count Shelley . . .

. . . Too numerous to mention!!!

The sound system has brought pleasure to many a Reggae lover in the Blues Dance . . . In the 70s one of the trends was for the D.J. to bawl out 'Who seh more cut'? To which the crowd replied 'Trouble it' or 'Go deh'. Upon this, he'd scrub a dub/tip a tone and bruk some bone with version galore by the score. And he who felt it, knew it!! It is in remembrance of that I wah, that I and I brethren hath created this I wah. Tune in!!!

Dennis Blackbeard Bovell

(Liner notes to the album, I Wah Dub
More Cut Records, RDC 2002)

The note quoted above was the initial inspiration behind this book. The quote is sufficient to describe the nature and intensity of the emotion as lived memory . . . Tune in!

CONTENTS

1

COURT HOUSE DUB ENCOUNTER

1

He reached the county court before his mother. He stood outside gazing at the building. His attitude was that of defiance, but deep within him a fear had already gotten hold of his stomach, was nibbling discreetly at his intestines, and his arse nervously twitched. He felt a sudden and collapsing sickness, as though he wanted to vomit. He leaned against the wall as he heard a voice next to him say, 'Wha go on, Michael?' He wasn't even thinking when the source of his strength returned in him and he answered roots fashion, 'Man cool.' He suddenly returned to the mould of his original attitude – defiance, and he felt confident for the first time that morning. He had hardly eaten when he had risen that morning. The sleep that stood on the precipice of his body was a tortuous and difficult one. He tossed and turned and woke up thinking he was in prison. He got out of bed and went to the toilet to pee. As he stood over the toilet his arse kept twitching. He felt if he tried to pee shit would come. He stood for five minutes over the toilet and couldn't pee. He then decided to shit. He sat down and immediately began pondering on the possibilities of what would happen to him in the morning. There was so much thought in his head that he could work nothing out, nothing vaguely resembling sense came into his head. His head was overwhelmed with thoughts of his parents and family, the life he was leading and an emotion that verged on tears each time he realised that he had no education, no trade, and in fact was staying with the mother of his friend. When all these negative thoughts flew up and beat his brain he rebelled with a positive image of himself – he was becoming a *hard* sound system operator. He could hold a crowd even though the sound man allowed him only fiteeen minutes play once every week.

'I man well surprised to see the I down here', his friend said. He was leaning over as he spoke and had a bounce each time a word came out of his mouth. He was no more than sixteen. 'I man reach down same way, Rasta', Michael responded, looking over his friend's shoulder to see his mother asking the attendant for what seemed to be directions. 'Well, is one ting I man want show the I and is the man supposed to let the I lawyer do all the talking, seen? The man suppose to be cool and act like a weepy youth. Just look like the man doan know wha go on, seen? The man have social worker? The I suppose to know that. Man must have him social worker talk for the I bout the I rough background and dem kind of tings dey. Still, man play it cool, like a respectful youth and man will cool. The man sight what the I a-try to show yo?'

'Yes, Rasta. The man show the I some tings, but still the I did know them runnings aready, yo no see it? Still, the I have to make some movements now, seen, because my mother a-forward. Sight her dey? Guidance still, Rasta.' 'Love, Rasta', the youth said and bounced down the corridor. Michael laughed to himself and felt immediately panic-stricken because he didn't know anything about a social worker. This was his first court appearance and although he had heard of his friends' vicarious and many encounters with the law, the force and power of the immediacy and intimidating environment of a court house, the trappings of its sedate power, the orderly and correct manner in which power was displayed, did not touch his imagination. He remembered the fear he felt each time he came into contact with a police officer, even a casual encounter as asking for directions, he became awed and overwhelmed by their presence. The first time he had seen the police responded to in the same brutal way they initiated was at a blues dance. It both frightened him and gave him power. He felt viscerally connected to the strength of the black youth who reacted as angrily as the police who were obviously hostile and animated by a spirit of war.

His mother came up to him, stood there looking at him for a minute and proceeded to tell him off. 'Boy, look at your shoes, you dont see it not tied. Look, there is yampey in your eye, you didnt wash your face this morning? You coming up before these people and you suppose to look decent and respectful, you know that?' As she was talking she was bending down to tie his shoe lace, then straightened out his clothes and handed him a tissue to wipe his eyes. 'You eat anything this morning? Come, let's go to the cafe across the road, boy.' Michael was thinking of protesting, but felt it made no use. Anything was better than this place, he felt. He walked slightly behind her, at her shoulder, while she was talking about the case he was going to face in half an hour. At times he felt he could hate his mother, but a deeper sense told him that was stupid because she still gave him things and showed care for him by checking up on him at least twice a month. It was his father he should really hate. He hated his father, but his feelings were ambivalent. A division ruled his heart: as a man his life could be understood as exemplary (he supported his family and occasionally beat his wife) because he was a trades man. As a plumber he could earn over a hundred pounds a week, but there was a dictatorial trait that he displayed that frightened and alienated Michael. If you didn't respond to the world and its demands as sharply as he did he would exercise no patience with you. His response was clear cut, you either did what you're supposed to do or forget it. In Michael's case it was *forget it*.

As they approached the exit a young black man approached them. 'Are you Michael Blumenthal?' Michael looked at the man puzzingly and said, 'Yes.' 'I'm from Griffiths & Co. The solicitors representing you. I'm the clerk. Listen, let's go inside and I'm going to ask you a few questions.' Michael's mother looked up and down at the man, as though she could not believe this young black man standing before her, casually dressed and wearing a tam could be a clerk in a solicitor's office. She almost sucked her teeth, but followed the man back along the corridor and onto some benches that were vacant. The more she looked at the man she could feel an inward laugh slowly building to explosion. It did not emerge, but broke her face into a smile – the contrast of her expression created a weird image of a shadow against a wall at night illuminated by candle light – she wore a serious expression even though her brown fattish cheeks pulled back against her will. Michael briskly glanced at his mother and a pain stabbed him in his chest. He felt embarrassed by her contempt and frightened by the man comprehending the meaning of her profile.

As they sat down the man pulled out a copy book. 'My name is Robert Johnson. I don't know if you've seen a barrister. I doubt it. But what I'm going to ask you will help the barrister put forward your case properly. Are you employed?'

'No, I'm not.'

'Do you live at home with your parents or not?'

'Well, I'm staying with some friends.'

'That wouldn't look good in court, so if your mother is prepared to say that you're still at home, it would look better before the judge.'

'Well, I don't want to get in any trouble. I mean I love my son and I spoke to him many times about bad company, but he won't hear. I don't know what's wrong with these children nowadays. I mean I can't go up there and tell lies. Suppose they find me out, eh?'

'Mrs Blumenthal, I understand your fears, right, but I can almost guarantee you that there would be no doubt about them finding out that he doesn't live at home. If you want to get the safest possible thing set up for Michael you will have to say he lives at home.'

'The police told me to plead guilty and they'll talk good for me.'

'Listen, don't mind what the police told you. That's their job – to convict; they're not going to speak up for you to get off. Why did they arrest you in the first place eh? If I were in your position, I would never plead guilty. I'm not forcing you to plead not guilty, but I think since you have no previous record it would be stupid to plead guilty when you have at least a chance of a suspended sentence.'

'You work for a solicitor?' Michael's mother was a little alarmed by this man's attitude to the law, but he spoke so honestly and confidently that she seemed to become convinced that he had her son's life at heart.

'Yes, Mrs Blumenthal. I hope you'll say he lives with you. He's only fifteen, you know, and it looks bad for a fifteen year old to be seen as a delinquent roughing it with friends.'

'O.K. I'll say that, O.K.?'

'Michael, you told me you're not working, right? Well, tell them you've been to several different employers over the last four weeks. If they believe you, they're gonna ask for a social worker's report which will mean you'll actually have to go back home and live with your parents . . . At least until his report comes in, you understand?'

'Well, I don't think his father want he back home, nah. Michael father done told him many times that if he want to leave school he should take up a trade, but Michael don't want to hear that. He want to take up with them bad boys and they all lead him astray. Michael got good brothers and sisters, you know. Is not the family he pick up all these bad habits from – is he friends and them, yes.'

'Yes, Mrs Blumenthal, but the point is even though your husband may not eventually take him back at least right now Michael has a chance of stalling them and your husband may change his mind. Look, I myself would talk to him if you think that would help.'

'Well, I don't know.'

'Michael, shop-lifting has become a serious offence in London, especially when it is black people doing it, you understand. I mean if you were an Arab or a middle-class white boy you would stand a chance, but you're young, black and unemployed, right. You're not at school, right. So they'll be looking at it from that angle, you understand. If the barrister decides to call you on the stand, don't get frightened, it's only people dressed up you're talking to. But you have to act respectful: bow your head slightly and look at the judge all the time. Don't stare him in the eye, but keep your face in his direction, right. Try and get his sympathy. There isn't much to this case, it's not going to take long, maybe twenty minutes maximum, O.K.?'

Mrs Blumenthal looked at Robert Johnson with suspicion and some emotional derision. She wondered what could this young black man do for her son, and this suspicion was reinforced by the past experiences she had had with black professionals. A black solicitor had acted for her in a court case involving a complaint against a white neighbour. She had only two meetings with the solicitor and one meeting with the barrister. When the case came to court the solicitor was not present, nor did he send a representative. The barrister conducted the case without an adequate defence and she had lost. Robert was fully aware of the object of incredulity he had become under Mrs Blumenthal's scrutiny. He in turn had developed an armour from which he was protected – he assumed a stance of quiet respectfulness and this eventually disarmed the client. Younger women found him fascinating because he was able to talk with a confidence and an assurance and a certain charm . . .

Mrs Blumenthal did not flinch when she recognised Robert had caught the expression on her face. 'So where is the barrister then?' she managed to ask.

'He should be here soon', Robert stated with an even tone.

'Did my son have a meeting with your barrister?'

'I believe so, Mrs Blumenthal', he lied.

'You don't sound so sure yourself. You telling me the truth?'

'Believe me, Mrs Blumenthal, you don't have any reason to be afraid.'

'Why you think so? My son could go to jail, you know. And you look a bit young to be handling this case. To tell you the truth, I don't have much faith in black lawyers nah. You know I lost a case because of them, and my friend paid all this money as a deposit to a black lawyer and you know the man was so stupid he didn't read the contract which he had in his office. And somebody just ups and buy the property she wanted. You tell me if that ain't bad business, eh?'

'I agree with you, madam. But because one or two black lawyers are negligent that doesn't necessarily mean that all are.' He knew he was telling lies, but he felt under the circumstances they were justified. In fact, Griffiths & Co. did not arrange a conference and he had to cover up his company's deficiencies. Mrs Blumenthal scowled and gave him a sharp look. She thought no wonder black people can't progress. They so inefficient. Robert understood Mrs Blumenthal's fears and felt she was justified in her apprehensiveness. Although she was right, he thought, there was another angle to it. Because of the boom in black people going to court and the parallelled boom in black community organisations, black solicitors and barristers tended to get most of the criminal work. This was because some black organisations referred cases to the black solicitors who in turn partly assisted the organisations financially. White solicitors were resentful of black ones because they were making money too rapidly. And when the whites received cases involving blacks they refused to brief black barristers. White barristers had also not demonstrated a boldness to attack the police or the judiciary for its inherent and displayed racism. Black clients felt betrayed and were usually sent down. Black barristers came to the rescue by making racism an integral aspect of defence in spite of its controversy and threats and attacks from the establishment. But when he looked at Mrs Blumenthal he felt we had a long way to go to dispel this justifiable distrust.

When the barrister came into the corridor of the court house, Johnson walked up to him and they exchanged words. The barrister then came over to Michael and they also exchanged words. They went over what Johnson had gone over with them, but the barrister was interested in the actual mechanics of the alledged theft, a phrase that he himself used when questioning Michael. It turned out out that Michael wasn't apprehended with anything on him. He was *seen* stealing by the Boots in-house detective. The friends who participated in the alledged theft all ran away, and when the store detective shouted 'Stop!' Michael stopped immediately. Perhaps it was the authority in the man's voice which reminded him of his father's that precipitated his standing on his usurped spot of earth. The barrister seemed optimistic – he could put forward the argument that because of the crowdedness of the store and the obvious youthfulness of the boys (he thought about saying black, but decided not to since the store detective was himself black) that the store detective must have mistakenly identified Michael as participating in the act with the other boys. The barrister who was a Guyanese Indian was very slow and deliberate in his questioning and exhibited a calm and confidence that made Mrs Blumenthal's eyes open: she was seeing black men in a professional context for the first time and something was happening in her insides. She felt an indescribable thrill that she could not explain. She had seen professional black people, but mainly in a capacity as clerks or insurance salesmen or very few teachers. And usually they were confined to working under white people from which they refused to identify with their black customer because of their preoccupation with reflecting a professional approach commensurate with what they imagined their white colleagues would appreciate – detachment.

When they left Court No. 3, Mrs Blumenthal could not believe it

She felt thrilled and happy and her fat cheeks pulled back from one side to the other showing her glistening white teeth. She thanked the barrister, shook his hand, talked badly about Michael, and was about to leave. The barrister felt it was his duty to talk to Michael. 'You're lucky this time, Michael. My job is not to determine whether you're guilty or not guilty, but to put forward my best defence. In this case there was clear-cut confusion due to the fact that other boys were involved. You also had the good sense not to say anything foolish. But you should let this be a warning to you – next time it would not be that easy. So your best bet is not to have a next time, right?'

'Yes, right.'

'You can smile now, boy.' The barrister laughed, Mrs Blumenthal laughed, and Michael and Johnson only smiled. Michael shook both the barrister's and the clerk's hands and they left. The barrister said to Johnson as they walked down the corridor, 'I can see that feller coming back to these courts. He seems like a confused boy – he has some kind of family problem.' Michael and mother walked out the court house, as they walked past the swing doors she started scolding and berating Michael. Michael's friend came up to him and said, 'The man cool?' Michael nodded while still walking. The boy said as Michael passed him, 'Seen, Rasta. I man got fined, but man cool still.' Michael didn't answer because his mother was already breathing hard. She pushed Michael by the left shoulder and he nearly stumbled. He was about to cuss her, but he controlled himself. He thought he wasn't living with them, so they had no rights to anything on him. But he just walked faster while his mother kept shouting, 'Michael. Michael. Michael. I calling you, boy.' He walked faster, thought about running, but kept his dignity by walking briskly and gracefully. But his mother could not resist running behind him, he could feel her deep-breathing upon him, and that was when he decided to spring. He ran quickly around the corner and onto a bus waiting for the lights to change. As he walked to the top of the bus he saw his mother flaring, lip pointedly, with fierce wide-opened eyes, a shrowd of blank staring disbelief and stunnedness marking the feeling in her heart. She just stood there at the lights, not even looking up at the bus, but at the imaginary figure of Michael where he had started running away from her.

Michael sat down, in front of him was an old white couple who started coughing and spitting into their *handkerchiefs*. He placed his palm over his nose and got up, walked to the front of the bus and sat down. The bus was going very slowly, the traffic was heavy for this time of day, and he looked down at the expanse of space before him as the bus climbed the top of the hill. He lit a cigarette and exhaled with a sign in response to the fleeting moments of freedom that he experienced watching the wide open streets before and on both sides of him. His mind was spinning like an *axis* and thoughts, like last night, flapped magically in his brain. He felt good that the barrister got him off. He felt exhilarated by this new understanding of how the law operated. He felt for a brief second immune to the police and the world around him until the gruff voice of the black conductress brought him back to reality, 'Any more fares? Any more fares'? His first response was to underestimate his ride. 'Ten pence.' The woman didn't take the money from him, but looked him straight in the eye and responded, 'Where you going, mate?' He thought for a second because he didn't know this part of town too well. 'The next four stops.' She took the money from him, sighed, clicked the fare, pushed the ticket into his hand, stood for a second looking at him, and walked away. He turned his head around and looked at the woman, looked at the woman whose figure was almost to perfection. She had a round high bottom and from the sides he could see her breasts almost perfectly shaped. She had a false bit at the back of her head tied with a mauve ribbon. He couldn't relate the voice, her still youthful years, beautiful figure, neatness, to the person he was actually watching at. He thought maybe she had a row with her husband or boyfriend last night.

The conductress came back up the stairs. Michael heard her voice and knew she was coming towards him. He sat in his seat and planned his moves. When she came beside him he rose up; she looked at him with her mouth half opened and Michael began to walk past her. The old white couple were still coughing and spitting. 'Wha wrong with you, woman? You can't see I done pay my fare already? Bloodclaat!' She didn't say a thing. She just placed her hand on the metal part of the seat where he was sitting, looked through the glass window and then swung her head back at him. When he reached the top of the stairs he looked back and she smiled broadly and a sound emerged from her throat. Michael couldn't help but smile too and jumped off the bus as it turned the corner. He didn't know exactly where he was and just walked along the street looking into shop windows. Each time he saw a police officer he quickly pretended not to see him and walked faster. He reached Trafalgar Square and went down the tube at Charing Cross. It was only 10.30. There was an attendant in a box at the entrance to the escalator and Michael wondered how he could dodge him. He waited until he saw a number of people passing and joined them. As they flashed their tickets at the attendant he walked quickly to the far side of them, kept his eyes on the escalator and went down. The attendant couldn't or wasn't in the mood to stop him. If he did he would have to allow the possibility of a lot more people walking through freely.

When he got to the platform he stood for a second, punched twenty pence for a Cadbury fruit & nut chocolate, and began to eat it rapidly. The Bakerloo line came in. He jumped on and walked through the carriages until he saw an attractive white girl. He sat down opposite her, lighting a cigarette and kept glancing at her. She was about twenty. She kept her eyes on the map of the tube while stealing glances at Michael. The train was almost empty and the girl kept discreetly looking at Michael glancing at her. At Piccadilly Circus the train began to full up and the girl got off at Oxford Circus. He rode the train all the way to Kensal Green, got off, paid the attendant fifteen pence and turned right into the Harrow Road. He was thinking of waiting for the 18 bus in front of the petrol station, but decided to walk up to Harlesden instead. He stopped outside Gangsterville Record shop and listened to some Reggae, but walked on. The sun was shining, but there were clouds in the sky, and suddenly without explanation the rain started dripping. In two minutes it stopped. The sun was still shining when Michael opened the door with his key. Tubbs, his friend, was home. Michael knew that before he came through the door because he could hear the sound of Reggae. Tubbs had built two three foot high speaker boxes, stuffed them with cloth and old carpet and had an eighteen inch speaker, a mid-range and tweeter into each. The sound was overwhelming in his parents' small two bed-roomed flat.

'Ey, Tubbs!'

"Yow, man! I man right here! Forward nah, man!' Tubbs turned the volume down and they slapped each other's palm. 'So the man cool?!'

'Yes, man. I man get off, you know. The barrister was hard no blood claat!'

'Yes, mi idren! But the man must cool still, seen? So wha go on inna the court?'

'I man sight a brethren – him name don't reach me still. But the I was letting me know the runnings. Still, I man was cool. The case didn't last too long, only bout fifteen minutes. But the barrister and his bredder, Robert Johnson, was well nice, man. Tell the I the runnings.'

'Wha bout the I modder? She forward?'

'Yes, but you know how it is. She started telling the I off and I man couldn't deal with that. So I man just tracks.'

'So wha she a-carry on with?'

'Nuff tings, Rasta. I man can't deal with that . . .'

'Seen, Rasta. But is love still, you know. The man's modder still love the I and it come out kinda possessive. I must tell the I he must deal with him modder, you see it?'

The conversation became too heavy for Michael. He couldn't relate to the talks that Tubbs gave him. He admired Tubbs as a main and skilful brother, but he couldn't respond to his reasonings when it came to the family. Tubbs had an excellent relationship with his parents. They never seemed to bother him. It was this thought that made him excuse himself. He went to the bedroom, took his shoes and jacket off and lay down. The thoughts of the day re-ran in his brain and he kept thinking of the black conductress. He was still thinking about her when he lost consciousness.

2

PRESSURE WITH FAMILY DUB

12

It was 6.30. Outside was still bright. There was life in the street. People were walking up and down, and young ones were standing on the pavement making conversation. In the living-room, Crossroads was on TV. Roberta, Michael's sister, never missed an episode. If she wasn't home on time, her mother watched it and told her the story, that is, on nights when Josie Blumenthal wasn't herself going to bingo with her Dominican friends. This evening Roberta was in the living-room sitting on the sofa, and between her thighs her youngest sister, Evelyn, was having her hair plaited into cane-row. Evelyn was a quick beautiful thing, the image of her father, and she had already mastered the art of being extremely gracious, endearing and a sweet little thing to her father whenever she wanted something. Ronald (all his friends called him Ronnie), Evelyn's mother said, spoiled the child. But the TV was on and the lives of Crossroads' people were peopling Roberta's head. Even if Evelyn wanted to talk, she couldn't. The brush in Roberta's hand would have come down upon her head.

Josie came into the room and sighed, 'O God. Girl, I tired, I really tired, yes. O God, girl! Girl, there was so much damned work today I thought that old bald-headed jewish boss woulda killed me. My back is paining me bad bad, and all my hands feel like I suffering from rheumatism.'

'O God, woman, Crossroads on nah!'

'O God, yes, Crossroads. I feel so tired I can't even think about that nah.'

'Well, let me watch the show, eh.'

13

Josie sat down, then rose again to take her coat off. She was one of those people who abosultely believed that England's weather was completely unpredictable and even though summer was officially here, she still felt convinced that the weather could suddenly change again. She always blamed her colds and those of her children and husband on the English weather. The English people themselves had a joke about their weather: you walked with an umbrella, a coat and a swimsuit. Josie was certain that the weather was to blame because she innoculated her family with cod-liver oil capsules and wheat germ in any form, and she always made a habit of keeping orange peel in case someone in the family came down with a cold. When she had taken off her coat she went into her bedroom. She put away her handbag and scratched her pubic area, then massaged her breasts. This was a habit she had since she was thirteen. She had a huge backside and breasts to titilate most men. She was short and plump and her complexion light brown. Back home they would call her a *red woman* and she had small splashes of what looked like lotha on her face. She was thinking of resting, but felt she should start cooking the food. When she entered the kitchen, she realised that Roberta had already put the rice on to boil, the seasoned meat was already cooking too. Roberta had already started peeling the provisions, but must have raced out to look at Crossroads. Josie was always satisfied by the fact that her first child was a girl and wasn't much of a problem to her. She peeled the rest of the potatoes, yam and dasheen and made a vertical cut into the green banana so that it would boil quickly. When she put them to boil, she went back to the bedroom where she saw a white enevelope on her dressing table.

She opened it (it wasn't stuck together), recognized it to be a school report and sat on the bed. Unexpectedly, all of Michael's subjects were O's except woodwork and art in which he received an A and B respectively. Josie was annoyed, but not dismayed. She took the report into the living-room and interrupted Roberta's program. 'All you see this?' She was waving the paper before Roberta's eyes. 'All you see this? Michael got O's and this time he even got a C in Maths. Could you imagine that! The boy did so well last year and even Maths which used to be his favourite subject, the boy doing bad in. Look at this nah!'

'Why you getting yourself so worked up. I left school at sixteen with two GCE's, and I'm working in a boutique. Paper don't mean nothin unless it is plenty paper. You know Michael doesn't like school, so I don't know why you getting so upset. Let's watch the show eh.'

'Roberta, Crossroads more important than your brother, eh? You pay more attention to that program than you pay to your damn brothers and sister.'

'O God, ma, you behaving like we can't discuss it when the show finish. Give me five minutes nah.'

'Look your father coming. Michael is wasting his own time pretending he studying and . . . and . . .'

'Michael tell you he pretending nah? He makes it quite plain that school is a bore, that he would rather leave than stay and mess around. I don't know why you get so excited, ma. Just leave the boy alone . . .'

"Leave the boy alone? You see what they write here? Michael is causing problems at school, disrupting the class with his loudness and they say he don't coperate with the teachers. The only good thing they have to say about him is his woodwork and art. But the boy can't get no work as no artist, all this Rasta thing he got all over the room, who will want to employ somebody like that to paint Rasta, eh?'

'He could make posters and sell, you know. Some of the boys do that. Even the white boys down Leicester Square and Trafalgar Square . . .'

'Make a living . . .? What kind of living you talking about? He might as well turn beggar, nah. You must be encouraging Michael to be the way he is, yes.'

Ronnie came into the living-room and took his hat off.

'Ronnie, you see what the teachers saying about Michael – that he disrupting classes and making noise and interfering with the other children. And the boy got all O's, even Maths which he used to do so good in, he even get a C for that. The only thing he do good in is woodwork and art. And this girl, Roberta, saying he could make a living selling Rasta posters in Trafalgar Square and Leicester Square. I say she encouraging Michael in he stupidness.'

'I already tell you what I think that boy should do – either he leave school and get a job or I want him out of here. I tired talking to that boy and he too big for beating. And if you hit your children in this country and they go to the police the police go lock you up for your own child and put him with some white people. I done talk.'

'But Ronnie, you don't think you should try with this boy, eh? We just can't give up on him like that. Why you don't talk to him seriously. He don't listen to me. I can't talk to him.'

'I go talk to him one more time, and I tell ya, if he don't listen to what I have to say, he will have to leave this house. I don't like to repeat myself too much. I can't talk forever. And I might just lose my temper and kill that boy. So I will talk to him tonight, eh, and that will be the last talking I do with that boy.'

'I can't even listen to my show.'

'The way you carry on with that show, you would believe you was acting in it,' Ronnie said, laughing. Ronnie left the room and Josie soon followed him still commenting on his school-report.

The sun was beginning to go down, but it was still clear outside. Michael still hadn't come home and it was nearly time to eat. William, Roberta's boyfriend, turned up at 7.15 and sat down in the living room. William, when he did come to the house, always timed the readiness of dinner. Roberta always teased him about this and she was going to but William anticipated her.

'Who cook food, girl?'

'You put money to buy nah, what you talking about food.'

'Is one money I put! My pay packet spent on this family.'

'But hear this boy eh?! People would think he really supporting us – the poor Blumenthals!' She laughed. ' These Trickidadians eh!' She could never overcome the novelty of listening to Trinidadians speak. What made it funny was the bold, crude, nasty sense of humour coupled with the pronunciation of words. She had met William about six months ago and they made steady companions. William made no secret of his pleasure in enjoying her curves. She was medium height, her mother's complexion and also had her mother's generously gifted body, plus she had a very attractive face. Her eyes were huge and they pinned any object to them. William felt magnetised by her eyes and broad thick lips two shades darker than her body. Her lips looked always moist and sumptuously suggestive.

'You staying home tonight?'

'Who would like to know?' Roberta answered and flicked out her tongue at him. He recoiled from the tremor of the shiver that went through his body. Her eyes opened wide and then squinted at him. He red with emotion. Roberta, he spoke to himself, really had total control of her body. She used every aspect of. her to devastating effect. He smiled and pulled his beard.

'Girl, you lucky you at home, yes!'

'What you woulda do nah?' She laughed again, narrowing and then expanding her eyes. The sensuality of her lips looked like golden tissues, swollen and warm. He licked his lips.

'You better be careful what you say in front of my *innocent sister, yes. You* know what you Trinidadians are like. Where is John and Sam?' She suddenly had her interest rivetted to her younger brothers. 'I haven't seen them since I've been home.'

'They're having their dinner, Roberta.' Evelyn spoke for the first time.

'You saw them having their dinner?'

'Didn't you see me go out a minute ago?'

'No. Well, that's alright. What happen to Michael, he aint come home yet?'

'I haven't seen him.'

'Why aren't you eating your dinner, Eve?'

'I aint hungry just yet.'

'You're never hungry until ma comes out with that strap for you. You better go and eat.'

'I don't want to . . . not yet anyway.'

'Eve . . .! You want your mother to come out here for your tail?!'

'I'm going.' She left the room looking sheepishly at William.

'Is you she want to stay here and ogle at, you know.'

'All little girls are like that. When I was her age I used to want to stay and listen and look at older women all the time.'

'Oho! You never did tell that to me though. You was a naughty boy, eh?'

'Girl, you could twist things. If it makes you feel happier – all to you.'

'I won't tell you what makes me happy . . .'

'Yes, that's because you're nasty and stink!'

'Me nasty and stink . . . Is you make me like that. Six months ago

I was an innocent little girl . . .'

'You innocent?! You was already a seasoned woman doing ya tings aready . . .'

This type of needling and two-party play she liked, but when it became close to her very self she became petulant and vexed. It was true that she had slept with one boy before she had met William, but the relationship wasn't important, nor did it last very long, nor did it have strong emotional ties. The boy had grown up with her since she came to England at the age of five. He was almost like a brother in emotional affinity to the entire family. As she blossomed he became curious about her body and desire grew strong in him. She allowed her breasts to be fondled by him since she was fourteen. They kissed only on the lips at that age. When she was sixteen they slept in the same bed together, hugged up tightly and fell asleep. But they never made love. Six months after her seventeenth birthday the same incident repeated itself. They went to bed intending to kiss, fondle and perhaps sleep. But the intensity of emotions and the insistence of his increasingly hot hands upon her breasts, his deep heavy breathing and the swelling in his pubic area, animated her own desire. He had fondled her breasts until the nipples felt hot and hard and she experienced tingling sensations in her neck and thigh muscles. He raised her jumper and kissed her nipples and bit them gently. He had never done that to her. The effect was startling. She almost pushed him away, but his insistent hot hands steadied her. Then his hands kept reaching lower down her body. She kept holding his hands, keeping them away from her pubic area. He kissed her ears and she giggled. He kissed her breasts again. It seemed like hours. Finally she allowed him to touch her. She giggled again. Then he was taking her panties down; she did not resist. He took out his penis and he struggled with her hand until he forced her to touch it. It felt like a piece of wood in her hand. She panicked and nearly rolled off the bed, but he was already on top of her, forcing himself into her. She felt a pain of indescribable cruelty. She felt like her insides would burst open. She pushed him off, but he came back again, groaning like a wounded animal. It felt like time would never come to an end. Finally, with pure exhaustion he stopped. He could not get into her unless he used real power and violence. A variety of conflicting emotions went through her: suppose her parents found out, suppose he had come in her, if sex is like this I never want to have it . . .

William turned the TV to another channel and there was a program about acupuncture. Evelyn came into the room and asked Roberta if she wanted to eat. Roberta got up and went out with Eve following. About a minute after they left Michael came into the living-room. He hailed William and sat down. He looked tired and dishevelled. He also looked worried, jumpy and in anticipation of something. William allowed him to catch himself before conversing.

'So everything cool, Mike.'

'No, Rasta. It dread. It dread out here, man.'

'That's life, you know, tings are tough.'

'But it could be better if man had understanding parents. They don't know what it like to go to school in this country. They think it's like back home with black teachers. These white teachers are dread, man. They racist. Them don't understand that.'

'You try talking to them . . . ?'

'Well, I did try, yes, but it difficult to explain to them when they can't understand the situation. Like, maybe back home school and the relationship like between the student and the teacher was like different. But it's different when you have white teachers making remarks about you: wog, nig-nog, monkey, and that kinda stuff. You should know, man, you went to school over here. You must understand what I'm talking about. You musta feel it . . . '

'I went to school over here for six years, yes, but I never identify with their racism. If you just allow what they say to get to you then they could defeat you. They used to tell me I was good with my hands, that I should be a mechanic or something. But still, what they say I know is bullshit. So I don't bother with them. I just did my work the same way. It's when they feel that they making an impression on you, then you start reacting to what they say. You understand? The time you should be working out your own thing you thinking about what they say and what they ain't say.'

'The man understand, yes, but like my parents aint understand that, man. I can't talk to them. My mother nags and nags and my father doesn't say much. If I don't do what he say he want to beat me up like I am some baby, man. I am fifteen, man. They can't treat a big youth like a child, seen? So them tings dey just throw me off, you understand.'

19

'Well, I don't know what else to say, Mike. The whole world is like that. People try to mess with your vibes, throw you off, but you have to keep stepping. You can't make them freak you out, man. I went through a lot of tings with my parents, too. You have to struggle with them for them to come to some kind of understanding. They just don't come on your side overnight, man.'

Roberta had a tray in her hand with food and a drink.The glass was in a coaster made of plastic and very colourful. It was the kind of coaster that William's parents had and betrayed a working class background. William hated the sight of it. The tray was a colourful one with designs of people dancing and it looked like it had seen better days. The carpet in the living-room was one of those hideously ugly swirly types and the walls had pictures of Jesus Christ having the last supper, calendars and little bird objects made from plaster of paris. These type of ornaments always made William feel uneasy, as though it reflected, in his mind, the profoundest attempt to inculcate the proverbial trappings of aspiring middle-class respectability – it was middle-class in the minds of the striving Caribbeans who could also exhibit the narrowest example of minds in their ignorant display of beliefs and ideas. He saw some do it in his own family and some in Roberta's, and he understood Michael's withdrawal from an identification that was both perilous and callously unthinking. And eventually led to oppression of the adventurous spirit – a spirit that was examining the very fabric of its own existence in the context of a foreign, imposing society.

When he looked at Roberta he saw something that most modern women did not have – a simple appearance, gold earrings, plaited hair, no make-up. A totally cultural woman with a connection to her past without being conscious of it. She winked at William and pursed her lips mockingly. He felt a wicked sensation burning at the back of his head. She placed the tray on his lap and gave Michael a stabbing suprised stare. 'Well, hello stranger. I thought you was dead, boy.'

'Why you thought that?' Michael liked his sister, but felt both jealous and resentment towards her. She seemed to be easily assimilated into the groundings of his family and was, as a result, loved by them, and simultaneously he resented her acquiescence to their named and unnamed rules. She didn't revolt against it. As young as he was he knew the only taboo that she really faced from them was her very sexuality, the possibility of them knowing that she could be endangered, and this in spite of them accepting the idea of a steady boy friend. 'Why I thought that eh? You know what time it is, boy? It's nearly eight o'clock. You didn't even come home from school. And wait until ma and daddy see you . . . You did really bad at school, boy, and they really disappointed and vexed by the way you keep losing more and more interest.'

'That is my business, man. I aint see what that got to do with you or anybody else.'

'Tell that to the mister up there,' and she pointed to the ceiling, 'not to the mister in the next room. He will wail your tail or send you out to join some of them mad friends you follow.'

'Come off it, Roberta. Which mad friends I have . . . You trying to say because man is Rasta they mad?'

'You know what I'm talking about. If a boy aint living nowhere and talking foolishness without backing it up, they must be mad. This is not the West Indies where we have sun all the time. Is winter and snow over here . . .'. Their voices were raised above that of the TV and their parents came out to see what was happening. Josie opened the door with a bang, closely followed by Ronnie. Josie looked frightened and apprehensive while Ronnie looked calm like a river. Sam, John and Evelyn followed. The room was now crowded and warm. William felt like an interloper in a family concern and was thinking of a legitimate way of excusing himself when Roberta cut her eyes at him, as though to make him aware that she was reading his mind.

'So mister now reach home eh?' Michael remained silent. 'Mister lost his tongue, eh? He cant talk. He cant say goodnight?' Josie was hotting up and her eyes were burning with anger. 'Hello, Mr Blumenthal,' William said and crossed his legs. The tissue he had in his hand was slowly being crumpled up in his fists. He ate half of the food already and picked the tray up to sit at the table, glad to get away from this family dispute. Ronnie nodded to him. Josie saw him, but it was like a blur. He appeared there and not there. Her energies were concentrated on Michael. Michael still didn't reply. His heart felt like a ton, fear was nibbling at his insides, he felt a thousand emotions go through his brain, and the vicissitudes of the English climate was experienced within his internal geography of feeling: from hot to cold to temperate to cold again. He felt fear surmounted by bravery, he was a boy struggling through a mountain landslide and a man climbing to the top...

'Michael,' Ronnie said with an authority that had no precedent. Michael came back to reality with a stunned open-mouthed wordlessness. Ronnie was his usual calm self. 'Michael, we saw your school report today and your mother was disappointed. I don't have many words to say to you. You know what my ideas is aready. I tell you aready that you either leave school or go and learn a trade. I could get you a job with me easy. If you don't like that you could try something that you like. Tell me what you like and we could start from there.'

'Well . . .'

'Ronnie, you don't see the boy ain't want to do nothin. He had even think about nothin . . . '

'Give him a chance, ma.'

'Well,' Ronnie said, 'what you say? Fair is fair, if you don't like what I suggest, then suggest a idea of your own, eh?'

'That boy need a good licking. He need a good licking to put some sense into him. That is what he want.'

'Come on then, Michael.'

'Well, I get a lot of pressure from school . . .'

'Pressure from school, pressure from school, you know what you talking nah? You hear the rubbish he talking. Roberta what pressure you get from school? This boy only making excuses, yes.' Josie was red with anger.

'Ma,' Roberta interjected, 'let Michael speak for himself. Calm down.'

'Calm down . . . ?'

'Well, I get pressure from school whether you want to believe it or not. Boys have it more harder than girls. They get more pressure from the teachers. They get more discriminated . . .'

'Roberta!' Josie exclaimed, 'What this boy talking about? Tell me, eh, because I know he talking stupidness.'

'I don't know myself. If the teachers racist, so what. That can't prevent you from learning if you want to.'

'Well, I can't get along with them sort of people. They call me names and all sorta things.'

'Well,' Josie said, her hands on her hips now, 'that ain't nothing new. You want me to come to the school with you? They been calling us nigger for a long time and sambo and all kinda names, so what? What that got to do with you? They can't prevent you from learning . . . '

'Well, I never feel like you all support me at all. You make me feel that I am doing wrong all the time.'

'Look, Michael, don't talk foolishness, you hear?' Josie was now screaming, rage causing her body to tremble and her face turn red and the veins stand out in her throat. 'Your parents don't support you! Your father tell you plenty times to leave school if you don't like it. You have a alternative: if you don't like school, take a trade, but no, you don't want that, you want to walk around the streets with your stupid Rasta friends and talk a lot of rubbish. That's what you want to do. You ain't want to work. No. That too decent for you. But if you can't hear you go feel. Mark my words, eh?'

'Michael, I don't want to lose my temper with you,' Ronnie said coldly and sternly, 'but this is the last time I ever want to speak to you about this, you hear? The next time I have anything to say to you is either I kill you or you kill me or you leave this house. If you is man enough to walk around with your Rasta friends playing you is man, you is man enough to go out on your own. As far as I see it you just wasting time. Is not me go feel it. I don't have no education. I could hardly read a newspaper, but I have a trade and I make good money. Nobody can't say I don't keep my family or I does beg or borrow from anybody, right? So if you can't listen to what your mother, your sister and me say to you, you better pack your bags and leave, you hear? I done talk.'

Ronnie left the room. William finished eating and belched discreetly. Michael sat in the armchair thinking the world was being eaten by a gigantic mouth and he was inside of it. A whole building being gobbled up within the jaws of a gigantic indescribable mouth. He felt panic, fear and desperation, but felt immobile, helpless and childish. Roberta felt sorry for him and could only express this with the painting of sorrow on her face. Josie was still talking and scolding, but Michael's mind was already trapped within the teeth of the gigantic mouth. The TV was still on and the children sat down feeling sullen and cold.

3

RUB IT INNA PARK/BABYLON DUB ENCOUNTER PART 1

Michael had gone out and returned when everyone was asleep. He went to the living-room and sat on the couch. He felt tired and disturbed. When he had left the house he had thought about seeing Tubbs, but felt like a baby unable to solve his own problems. Instead he just walked around, met some friends and drifted with them and finally returned home. He didn't put the light on when he came in but just sat in the darkness pondering on his next move. His whole being was preoccupied with his father's reaction to him and his mother didn't help with her relentless banter and scoldings. He felt alone and isolated from the weight of a deadening world around him. He felt he was totally on his own and no one and nowhere to go. He felt like a river surrounded by banks but unable to reach them in normal circumstances until the fury of the river flooded over onto the banks. He didn't feel the emotional fury necessary to provoke his parents into real consideration of his predicament. It was as though he had already given in to the inevitable choice he felt he must reach: leave home! But the thought of it flooded him with a fear and a dread he understood from the tightening muscles in his stomach, the feeling of nausea that slowly engulfed his head, then he felt himself spinning into blackness . . .

It was weird that afternoon (it seemed like afternoon because it was summer and light spilled over like magic) almost a year ago when he was walking past the pub. A black man who looked like six and a half foot was followed out of the pub by two white men. The man came out walking with a leisurely pace but clearly glancing over his shoulder at the two men. The black man's eyes were red, yet he didn't look drunk. The white men were clearly drunk. They were both drifting about, cheeks red, hair dishevelled and they still wore their dirty work clothes. One of them was saying something to the black man, but Michael didn't hear the first sentence fully.

". . . over here and rough up my . . ." The black man now stopped walking and turned around to face them both.

"What you going to do about it, mate?" the black man asked them.

"You can't come over here, in my country . . . "

"You're a fucking immigrant just like me mate. You come from Ireland. If you want to do something, do it."

"Looking for fucking trouble, are you, then you're gonna fucking get it, mate. You can't talk to my friend like that, you black cunt." The black man punched him in his face without saying a word. The other man looked at the thick heavy beer glass he held drunkedly in his hand. The black man punched him and the glass to the ground and kicked him in his stomach. People were gathering around. There was four black youths, a black man and a black woman dressed in a short skirt and black tights and wearing a wig, a drink in her hand. There were about ten whites. The first white man came in drunkenly and swung wildly at the black man who simply held the man's punch and slammed him against the wall of the pub. Then a small pen knife appeared in his hand and he cut the white man across his face. It was a surface cut, deliberately minor but sufficiently impactful to mark from just under his ear to the tip of his nose and to draw a profusion of blood. The man on the ground was groaning like a dog and talking into his hands. No intelligible words could be understood from him except when he cussed or talked about 'Jesus! Holy mother virgin' or some variation of the theme. It looked like he refused to get up. The black man clearly was not upset, fearful or in the least concerned about the injured men. A skinny drunken looking white woman with a stained white blouse drifted over to the black man and said, "The bastards deserved what they got!" She held on to the black man's arm while another white man came over to him. "You better get a move on, Bill, the coppers will soon be here." The black man smiled and started walking up the street with the white woman still holding on to his arm. She was drifting and walking dangerously and talking loudly, but nothing was understood except when she vehemently shouted "Bastards!" The black man turned around when he had walked about fifteen yards and looked back: the cut white man was picking up his friend from the pavement but he was struggling with his helper. "Leave me alone, get the fuck away from me!" He kept repeating these words while the man's blood now spilled on to his struggling friend. He took his filthy looking hand and wiped his face and it started to bleed even more. The black man waved to his white friend and walked up the road with his drunken white woman still cussing and screaming "Bastards!"

He thought then that he would always live with this demonstration of *dread* and fearlessness. He had never thought that a black man could be that bold and aggressive. This symbol of strength and power would come back to him in his dreams and when he confronted a violent situation.

Michael emerged out of the blackness feeling as though he was travelling through an endless tunnel and the frightening spreading feeling of claustrophobia precipitated a response from the consciousness of his dream that he came awake with a kind of anguished violence. For a moment he wondered what he was doing in the living-room, on the couch, then the memory came back to him, flooded him and he felt despondent and alone. The conversations of the evening came back to him like a shot and he felt hot all over, then cold, then he started cussing voicelessly in the fullness of his skull. For a moment his mind was blank then desultory thoughts came into and left his mind. He was trying to find a focus, unselfconsciously, but nothing settled, just the ruminating travelling pangs of fear that conctracted intermittently. Then he remembered. It was something, a model or phantom figure, that instructed him about the sultry condition of this town.

The first time he had seen her was when he had just entered secondary school. What brought his attention to her was that she was talking to the young girl like she was an adult. This startled him because his own parents had never spoken to him like this and he kept watching the woman and the daughter while they were shopping and surreptiously followed them, listening to their conversation. The girl was probably about his own age or a year older and she acted with a maturity that surprised him. The woman was talking to her daughter about their next-door neighbours, and their predilection for noisiness and their ability to drop words about her husband who it seemed had now left her. Michael did not know for what reason, but he subsequently saw the woman and the girl infrequently but regularly, usually shopping. Then for about a year he did not see her and got an atomic shock response when he saw the woman neatly dressed talking loudly to herself and the girl was not accompanying her. He felt like running up to the woman and asking her for the girl, but the suddenness of the thought made him aware of its stupidity. But he remembered feeling the shock of it and he talked about it with his sister. He then saw the woman often, always with a shopping bag in her hand and talking to herself. As time passed she began to dress rather gaudily. She wore extremely red lipstick, short jumpers, knee-length socks, gaudy looking costume jewellery and skirts that progressively got shorter and she always had the shopping bag in her hand, then she started wearing black rosary-like beads long like a rope wrapped several times around her neck. She remained like this at all times. She stopped talking, loudly or silently, to herself and merely walked the streets with a deliberate speed as though she had a destination. The thought of the woman, from happiness with a daughter she related to like an adult, to a woman who had 'lost', as Keith Hudson had said in his song, 'all sense of direction .! . . . had brought about in him a placement of his own predicament and it was as though he would always keep the memory of this woman at the center of his brain as a focus and a measurement of his own life and its steadfast progression to aloneness and perhaps isolation. "I am a blood claath Rasta!" The vehemence and violence of the thought in his brain in his magnetic-like fight against the woman's madness and cesspool of his own situation suddenly sprang forth a statement that he felt would always serve as a defence against disintegration and collapse.

He was pounding his fist into his open palm with grinding power and strength when he came to the realisation of what he was doing. He stopped. Then he laughed, put his hand to his forehead and rested against the couch. The tiredness was leaving his body and the intensity of his emotions began to recede to calmness. He was smiling now and the picture of the black man on the TV program acting as a Jamaican and speaking lines he thought unbelievable broke the tightness of his face. Relentless flashes of the man's face, his eyes opening like an inflated balloon and the way he pursed his lips and the way he uttered his lines . . . 'Mr. Jones, I was thinking, Sir, if you could excuse me . . . ' The thought of it calmed him and he fell back to sleep.

It was lunch break and some of the kids were going home, but about six boys followed three girls to the park. The summer day was beautiful, the grass smelled fresh and lovely, the little sun flowers looked yellow and light, and there were people sitting on the grass, children running about and kids playing football. At the other end of the park to the left there was a kiosk that sold soft drinks and ice cream. The six boys and girls had broken up in different directions. Two of the boys went to join friends playing football, another one went to chat up a girl, while another went to the toilet, which now left Jos and Michael and the robust-looking black girl, Bunting. They went past the kiosk and into the garden lined with benches. There were a few pigeons pecking at peanuts thrown by an old white man with horn-rimmed glasses. A black woman was reading a newspaper and there was a couple of old women chatting. They walked past these people and went behind the little Chinese-looking building that stood at the top of the garden. Jos was chatting up Bunting who was eyeing Michael with a thrown hint of an invitation, but Michael resistant and shy. Jos was a tall skinny light-skinned boy with curly hair. He looked like a product of black/white union, but he was in fact a mixture of Afro-Asian of the Caribbean. He was older than Michael by a year and a half and had a bad reputation with girls. It seemed almost all the girls at school had a fancy for him and he made the most of it. Most of the girls were moved towards him because of his complexion and curly hair, and the middle-class nice-boy image he projected at times through his mode of dress.

But Jos was the kind of boy who would utilise any aspect of his person to get what he wanted, but he wasn't particularly middle-class in attitude except that he had no value for money or clothes. Right now he wanted to fuck Bunting who seemed willing but playful and who still gave Michael that dazzling enchanted eye.

"So what you say, Bunts, you game?" Jos asked her smilingly.

"I don't know what you mean . . ."

"Oh come on, you not stupid, are you?"

"I might be."

"What, you don't fancy me then?"

"I didn't say that."

"You don't have to say, I can tell."

"You can tell what?"

"Bunts," Jos said and giggled, "what you want me to do, beg you?"

"Beg me for what?"

"You really want to know?"

"No. Don't tell me."

"Well, I'll see ya, yeh, you're fucking around, man."

"Well, I never tell you to go, did I?"

"You can say that in more ways than one, can't you? You don't have to say that in words. You want me to go?"

"Jos, the trouble with you . . ."

"Yeh, the trouble with me is that I don't have patience with the likes of you. You're time-wasters, you are."

"Don't be like that."

"Give me a kiss."

He leaned over and kissed her on the cheek. Her hands were at her side. She didn't struggle or resist. He kissed her lips but her cheeks didn't make any movement. She was as still as a spot of earth. He drew back, laughed and walked away.

"See ya, Mike. As for you, young woman, I man check you later."

"You're a good friend, aren't you?" Bunting shouted at him as he walked down the garden path. Michael had been studying the outline of Bunting's body. She had a longish face but full lips and very small ears. Her chin wasn't pointed, but roundish, and they hung over breasts that pointed out and into her nose. This astonished Michael when he realised that this five foot girl had such immaculately huge breasts. Her torso tapered into a small waist but her arse was flat and broad and her legs weren't particilarly impressive. The gleaming shiny hue of her blackness excited Michael. Her skin shone like newly varnished leather. He almost hiccupped when Jos had kissed her and her lips had involuntarily parted when Jos pressed against her: the thickness and rudeness of their shape!

"See what kind of friends you have, Michael". She said, breaking the silence. Her sudden words in the short interval felt like a stone had hit the building. He remained silent for two seconds.

"You know him better than me."

"No, I don't. What give you that idea?"

"Well, I've seen you two together chatting more than once."

"That don't mean nothin. I'm talking to you now, what does that mean?"

"Well, maybe you're right, but I man just thought . . ."

"You're one of them I man too, eh?"

"What d'you mean?"

"You're a Rasta, right?"

"Who says so?"

"I'm asking, that's what."

"I could be . . ."

"Yes, but are you?"

"What is it to you?"

"I just want to know, that's all, is there somethin wrong wid that?"

"You don't have to shout like we're having a fight."

"I didn't mean to, you know, it just came out . . ."

"Yeh, well, it's alright."

"Don't you have a girl-friend then?" She opened her eyes widely throwing them down to the ground and quickly glancing at his pants' middle. He never saw what her eyes actually accomplished, but he felt a pang when her eyes were thrown open so widely.

"Why d'ya want to know?"

"God! Can't I ask you a decent question widout having a reason?"

"Yeh, sure . . ."

"Well then, do you or don't you?"

"Too young . . ."

"Too young . . . ? Don't make me laugh! I bet you had a girl before . . ."

"No. I never." He immediately regretted saying that, but it emerged involuntarily, and he looked at the light clouds in the sky.

"That's a surprise. I've had a boy-friend."

"Yeh, and what happened to him?"

"Well, we sorta finished like."

"Why?"

"He was getting too serious." Michael knew she was lying. The boy was called Anthony and like most boys his age they were after the girls and then dropped them after discovering the source of their initial attraction. But he pretended that he didn't know.

"Really?" He smiled and cracked his knuckles, a habit he picked up from his father. Then he scratched his chest. Bunting opened her eyes widely again and looked down and up from the ground glancing at his pants once more. "Yes, really. You sound like you don't believe me, not that it matters."

"Why shouldn't I believe ya? You wouldn't lie to me, would you?"

' I bloody would!" And they both laughed and leaned forward slightly to each other, Bunting striking him affectionately on his arm.

"Don't you fancy me?" She asked this question boldly feeling the timing was right. "Don't tell me you don't. Bad for me ego!" They laughed again and she struck him on the shoulder once again, and Michael felt that he was really liking this wild girl. "Go on then, tell me you don't!" She laughed again and Michael looked at the marvellous apples that stood out beneath her shirt which now bounced up and down as she laughed. He felt tempted to touch and stroke them and bite them on the nipples. He shivered as these thoughts came into his mind. As she laughed her cheeks pulled back to her ears and her mouth widened and he saw her tongue like an attacking vulture stabbing at his ear and neck. "Go on then, kiss me. Let's see if you really fancy me. He laughed and he felt stupid standing there watching her. He looked around to see if anybody could see him. Across from him, over the fence and through the hedges, he could see the tennis players. In front of him he could see the double-decker bus as they passed and could hear voices but couldn't see people from the street. "Don't worry, you're safe here." She came right up to him and kissed him gently on the lips. Her lips felt warm and he kissed back feeling the nipples on her breast harden and prick his chect. She must be wearing those thin nylon bras, he thought, because he could feel her breast almost nakedly against his skin. When he kissed her back she threw her tongue into his mouth and the middle of his pants stiffened. She now had her arms on his shoulders and he felt himself drawing back from her so that she couldn't feel his penis, but she rested her hands firmly on his shoulder as if to tell him to remain there, simultaneously, she imperceptibly drew herself nearer to him. His penis gave a sudden leap in his pants that it struck against her lower stomach. She sighed when she felt it against her. He felt his face grow hot and red and a little apprehensive about the openness of their encounter. She pressed herself right up against him and shifted herself so that she could feel his penis closer to her vaginal area, but it struck against her upper thigh and she sighed again. Then she remained still and quiet except her mouth was making noises as she flicked it all over the inner parts of his mouth. Then she suddenly pulled away and looked down quickly at his pants. He felt stupid with the bulge there and didn't know what to say. She didn't say anything either, but just sat down on a bench under the building. He sat down and they remained in silence hearing the tennis ball being struck backward and forward and the laughter, noises and chat of the people inside and outside the park.

When his syes flew open he saw it was his sister prodding him on the chest. I must have fallen asleep again, he thought, and blinked several times before coming awake. His sister was talking to him, but he could not decipher a single word except the perfumed feminine smell she had. She was wearing his pyjamas again. "Wake up, Michael, wake up. You know what time it is? It's nearly five o'clock, you know that? Boy, what you doing in this sittingroom with no blanket and pillow, you don't feel cold? Come on, Michael, come, let's go to bed". Roberta had found him in here at least twice before and she used to tell him when he was quite young he always used to fall asleep quickly in the livingroom. It was a habit he must have cultivated unconsciously. Michael had always felt this room comfortable, warm and quiet, beyond thé domain of all others, particularly at night with the house asleep.

He sat there with his mouth open, his eyes fixed into space, then wiped his mouth with the back of his palm. "Michael, it's five o'clock, boy." He listened to her and wondered why she was getting so excited. Then he remembered that Roberta always showed this excitement when he slept in the livingroom. The events of last night may have precipitated her concern to an even greater degree. He smiled half-heartedly and Roberta's eyebrows suddenly pulled towards the top of her forehead as if to say: *what is wrong with this boy? Is he mad?* But instead of expressing the thought that spontaneously came into her mind her face expressed a simultaenous smile, and Michael giggled. He wiped his face again and scratched his head. It was thick and uncombed. He was about to say something when Roberta began to speak. "I don't know if you been thinking this ting over, Michael? But I have. Michael, you listening to me? I've been *thinking* . . . after last night I *know* tings are going ta get worse. You and dad are goin ta cross swords and it won't be nice. No. You should think about living with somebody, you know. I know you young, but you not really stupid even though you act like it to people. Maybe, you can stay with uncle Eggerton. You and him seem to get along alright, ain it? If you want me to talk to him, I could, you know. I could. Michael, do you understand how serious this ting is goin ta be? I don't know if you realize or see the danger of staying here with dad and mum with your attitude. I know you don't agree that you have a attitude, but anybody would say so if you hell bent on doin ting your own way. So, to me, is either uncle Eggerton or somewhere else where you can stay. I would personally feel better if you stay with uncle, because at least everybody will feel easier, more at rest, than if you leave home like you plan to. I can see it in your eyes, Michael. You tinking about it a long time, but more so since last night. You can't fool me, Michael."

Bunting slapped the girl in her face. The girl raised her hand in retaliation, but Bunting pulled her by the hand and threw her to the ground. The crowd of kids surrounding them was like that of a football match of rival supporters. They were screaming, clapping and laughing. Some teachers passed the fight and walked straight on. When the girl fell to the ground Bunting choked her neck, then scratched her face. The girl struggled and got hold of Bunting's finger in her mouth and refused to let go despite the heavy hammering of her head against the ground. Bunting's finger bled and her violence increased, tears streaming down her face. The crowd still applauded, screamed and laughed. Michael, standing and watching, could take it no more. He placed two fingers of each hand into the girl's mouth and pulled her mouth apart. Bunting was about to attack the girl once more, but Michael pushed her away roughly and simultaneously slapped her. The noise of the crowd stopped. Now they were murmuring. A boy came forward and started cussing Michael who, without saying a word, punched the boy in the stomach and kicked him. The beaten girl was dishevelled and bleeding and scratched up and her friends took her away despite her lame protestations. Michael now held Bunting by the arm and walked her away from the now loudly murmuring crowd. Bunting, still in a rage, cried, her chest heaving up and down.

It was four o'clock and the sun was out. They just walked wordlessly, Bunting following Michael's footsteps. Michael was two paces ahead of her and she just followed him. They were back in the park and Michael pointed to the tap for her to wash her face. She obeyed silently. She placed her finger beneath the cold water and the congealed blood turned to dripping. She washed her face, then wet her handkerchief and rubbed her neck, rinsed the hankerchief and tied it around her finger. Michael did not wait for her, but walked on over to the little building where they first came that rainy day. He sat on the bench and looked up at the sky. The thought of two girls fighting made him mad. He felt he could punch Bunting in her face for embarrassing him like that. Even though he showed little external emotion, his insides were turning up. She walked up the pathway and he could not help but gaze at her beautiful chest protruding through her clothes. The sight of her placed a calm over him despite the rising emotion in his chest. Bunting was thick, the flesh on her body stood out like a trained athlete. He liked the idea of a strong, robust girl. The thoughts of her strength excited him. She came up and sat down next to him. She had fixed her dishevelled hair and her face looked clean even though a slight swelling showed on her right cheek. They said nothing to each other for a long time, Michael cracking his knuckles like his father. Then suddenly Bunting began to talk, very heatedly. "She's a bitch, that fucking girl! She went telling people that I was going around with every girl's boyfriend and that I wanted to take her boyfriend away from her. Could you imagine that? That ugly bitch thinking I could be after her horrible boyfriend. That Keith is a sly cunt. He is such a fucking square, he is, what could I do with him!? She must be out of her bleeding mind! I shoulda broke her fucking neck, I should

. . ."

"Calm down, Bunting, calm down. I man can't take all that kinda talk."

"Why did you stop me? I wanted to kill that bitch. And you had a nerve pushing and slapping me like I was your child. I shoulda spit in your face!"

She laughed when she said this and flashed her eyes at Michael as though imparting another meaning. Then she smiled.

"Why didn't ya? That would be nice for ya – another fight."

"Well, seeing that it was you, I didn't want to embarrass you like. A girl beating a boy won't be that nice, would it? All your girls . . ."

"What girls? . . ."

"Don't tell me that you still don't have a girl?"

"Not unless you giving me one."

"Well, I am. Don't you see?"

"Too young for me . . ."

"You must be joking! I'm nearly fifteen, might I remind you!"

"So what? That don't mean nothin."

"I have experience."

"Oh yea."

"God, you're a funny bloke."

"Let's go, Bunting."

"Let's go for what? I'm staying right here!" Michael got up and was walking away, Bunting rose violently and banged her hand against the bench and uttered a sigh of disgust, and followed him down the pathway.

For two weeks he tried to avoid her. He would always be walking with his male friends and pretend not to see her. Almost every afternoon she waited at the corner outside the school yard, but he walked straight past as though she were invisible. She watched him apprehensively and sulkily. Her eyes flashing dangerously and her lips dramatically pursed. He watched her, his eyes either on the ground or in front of him, but flashing surreptiously at her. Then one day he almost bumped into her. She was glad for the excuse to speak to him, but when the words came out, they were with violence and hatred. He just looked at her and didn't say a word. Four months later she dropped out of school when she became pregnant. He was both relieved and alarmed: she was bent on self-destruction.

Her raging sexuality was immediately apparent and available. When she fancied a boy, she gave herself, and like an animal she looked for new prey. But there was something deep and disturbing he felt she had buried deep within the recesses of her soul and that she would not part with. He had several guesses, but none was certain. That was the last he had heard of Bunting.

Michael went to bed and was awoken two hours later by his father. His father told him the inevitable: leave the house. But his mother came in the room and pleaded for him. Michael went back to sleep and fell into a dream. It was a broken down old house and people were dancing, smoking and drinking. The music brought a deeply-felt happiness to the people's hearts, as though they were expressing a feeling that was buried within them, that had its genesis in some unknown oppression and as it surfaced a crushing weight fell and the gleam of a feeling rose up through their skins. The music was hypnotic, a simple repeated bass riff throwing out an unknown un-named magnetic power. The faces of the dancers were trance-like and as the music played it seemed that they would follow it wherever it led them. But it was Michael who was the sound system operator. It was he who was responsible for the feeling that came upon the dancers and his mind, like the dancers, was rivetted to the exorcised mystical qualities expressed by the music. He danced on an invisible floor. This happiness was abruptly destroyed by a bomb-like explosion and blazing fire and the faces of the dancers turned to horror and dread. He woke up almost violently and looked at his watch on the floor and it was nearly two o'clock. Roberta had left the curtains closed for him to sleep. The house was quiet. His father had probably gone to work, Roberta and his mother went shopping, and the kids gone to the park. He placed his hands underneath his head and rested against the pillow. The decision has to be made today, he thought. Thoughts came up like a lottery. The possibilities were there, but he could not decide which was to be embraced. Uncle Eggerton was a nice man, but he didn't want to stay there because his mother would be over there all the time. He decided he would bathe and then take a walk up to Harlesden.

He must have been standing at the record shop for an hour, watching as young people bought records and walked back out, and thinking he would like to afford records one day. The girls who bought records were all beautiful. There was no stereotype of the kind of black people who bought records from this shop: Indian, Afro-Indian mixture, and a variety of shades of black. When the music played a world of feeling came up in him and possessed him. Tubbs came in, bopping from one side to the next. "Hail the man;" Tubbs said, slapping Michael's palm. Across the street a police van came slowly to the corner. Michael watched it suspiciously. "Hail I", he answered.

"The man cool still?"

"Yes I", Michael said.

"What the man a do?"

"Just a check the sounds, I".

"Well, mek we tek a walk down by Jetstar nuh?" Michael agreed and they chatted easily. Michael's heart felt lifted. He felt easier meeting Tubbs. It was strange, each time he went out by himself, he felt like an alien. He felt he was constantly under scrutiny by other people, that he was under their observation at all times. This made him feel both self-conscious and fearful. His body tensed and tightness gripped his head, his muscles contracting with tension. Then when a face he knew came towards him his body instinctively responded with a release of tension and relaxation came into him, and an aliveness, a feeling of part of the world, came back to him like a shot. The magic within him immediately came back to life. He never did work out that his eternal expression – fear and bad-temperedness stamped on his face like a flag, was what made him the object of people's stares. It was a realisation that would come in adulthood.

"I man check a blues dance last night, Jah Mike, and it was hard no rass!" When Tubbs called him *Jah Mike* he felt like a grown up and respected. Tubbs was his only senior friend who made him feel part of a movement, an extended group of brethren. "Me a tell you! It was rammed, mi idren. And daughter! I can't tell the I when I last check a blues dance that had so much daughter. I man take a rub – rub-a-dub-style! Cha! Irie! Shaka play some wicked dub, well hard, iya. The man miss a tough set, me a tell yo!"

"Where it keep?"

"Bravington Road, Rasta. Off the Harrow Road. It was a bloodclaath abandoned house. The people move out last week and man just capture to make a money, yo no see it? It well nice though. So what the man do last night?"

"I man had an argument with my parents . . ."

"That no nice, Rasta. Man should reason still."

"School tings. Different runnings still. Like them tink is either school or trade, but man have to have time to work out in him head what him really want to do, seen?"

"True, true."

"But it always come to some big argument. I man can't get no overstanding. Last night they threaten is either I man come on like scholar or take a trade. And this morning the I did try to work out some tings and I man fall asleep in the livingroom, but the I sister, Roberta, did wake I. So I man went to bed this said mornin and they wake the I up, want throw I out. I man only fifteen and can't get no overstanding, yo no see it? I don't know what I want do. I man just can't cope with everything. School is a bloodclaath drag. I man can't deal with racist bloodclaath teachers. Is only the sound I man a check. I man have a feeling say that the sound a go do it for the I, seen. So I man want get involved inna it, seen?"

"Man overstand, Jah Mike, but the I coulda get a family to reason with the I parents, seen? Reasoning bring enlightenment, yo no see it?"

"Tubbs, you don't know them as I man. Sometimes I man feel that borstal woulda do it for the I . . ."

"What the bloodclaath you a chat! Borstal pussyclaath! I man tell you say that borstal is for the unrighteous. If man don't have no alternative . . . If man sentenced to a time dey, then I man understand, but Borstal more than the I parents . . . No sah, I man don't see no reasoning behind that."

"Well, I man check it different still, seen?"

"Jah Mike, the man must know what experience mean, seen, then the I can talk. Man have fe grow up and come man, seen, and tek on responsibility, seen. So what the I parents a do is to train the I from youth for responsibility, seen? But if the man feel say that you don't want stay, I man will take to I parents still, seen?"

"Tubbs, I man well appreciate that. Just so that the I can work my problems out, seen?"

"I man don't know what I parents will say still, but I man will speak to them for the I, seen? I man have him own room as the man know and I man don't mind sharing it with a brethren still, seen. But listen, Jah Mike, the man a Rasta? I man never check the I on that yet, seen?"

"I man still a check it out still, seen? I don't fully get up in the higher overstanding, but I man will like to go inna it and find out more what it a deal with, seen?"

"Well, I man will tek you by some brethren who are elder rastas, seen? The I them don't follow the church, cause the man structure carry the temple, yo no see it? Man worship inna himself to God. But the brethren them can reason with the I better than I man, so man can get up inna it, the higher philosophy, yo no see it?"

"Seen, seen."

They were so much involved in their conversation that they went straight past Jetstar and some young people were shouting to them as they went pass. Suddenly, they became aware of a general noise behind them and turned around instinctively and together to look at the brothers waving and shouting to them. They both laughed and said "Bloodclaath!" and Tubbs added "Selassie I!" Today being Saturday the street was filleld with people shopping. Harlesden has a sizeable number of blacks and they could be seen in varying ages making their way around this little town. It was also known that the police had a few undercover agents who prowled the streets checking out the primarily young people who had a reputation for theft and petty crime. They also made their presence felt by cruising in their cars or vans, possibly to induce fear into the youth. Tubbs and Michael crossed over the street and walked into Jetstar record shop to be greeted by handslaps by the brothers. The blacks who owned the shop never encouraged black youth in the shop because of the police angle, and though the music was exicting for the youth, the proprietors did not cater exclusively for them. They would play Soul/Funk, Jazz/Funk, Calypso, Highlife/Juju and adult music as well as Reggae. The youth characterised American music as "fockery" and could barely tolerate Calypso. There was now about eight youths in the small shop. They were either Rastas or wearing tams. The black man behind the counter was already expressing visual signs of apprehension. If the proprietors came in they would hold him responsible for the youth being in there. He was playing a record for an adult, stopped the record, and asked the youth if any of them wanted to buy a record. A youth said, "Let the man spin the record them then he would know what we want, seen?"

"Look, if you don't want nothin you can't stay in here, right."

"But how", the same youth said, "we gon know what we want if you don't play it? We just want hear what new sounds you have."

"If you not buying records, don't hang around, right. I just doing my job, right."

"Cha, man, this is", said another youth, scowlingly, "fockery."

"Leh we forward, man. These *men* them discriminate against they own black people. I bet if a whole bunch a white people walk in here, they would never tell them to leave and all that fockery they keep up with we, seen."

"I just doing my job, right." The man spoke quietly as if he were ashamed.

"Is a wonder him no call up the police on him telephone."

"Nah, them man so sophisticated, them have wrist radio to bloodclaath!"

"I man know say they have contact with police, seen."

"Leh we cool, the man only obeying him orders, seen. Leh we don't put no heat on the brother. It wrong still, but mek we forward." It was Tubbs' voice of reason that precipitated their movement out of the shop.

"Bloodclaath!"

"Selassie I go deal wid them bloodclaath. Them go have fe answer to the most high, seen."

As they emerged outside there was a crowd of people, black, white and Asian, and they moved instinctively to see what was happening. The police had just arrested a black girl for shop-lifting, it seemed, and she was protesting about being wrongly arrested. The police were telling the people to move away, but they stood their ground, and an Asian man came out of the shop and gave the police a shopping bag with materials in it.

"I didn't do nothin, man. I didn't steal nothin. I'm telling ya. There was another girl next to me and she dropped the bag and walked away when she saw that man coming towards us. I don't even know her. It wasn't me I tell ya."

"Look, you were seen by this man, right, so you're being arrested. If the evidence don't point to you then the magistrate will let you off."

"Magistrate? What you talkin about. I ain't done nothin. I ain't never been in trouble before, I swear."

"We're taking you in."

"Why you don't leave the bloodclaath gul alone."

"You're interfering with the course of the law, mate."

"What bloodclaath law you're talkin about – you just using strong-arm tactics to fuck-up the community."

"Go home, mate, will ya or I'll have you in jail."

"Leave the bloodclaath gul, man."

"Yeh, leh she go, man. You can't see you got the wrong person."

Another policeman walked over and grabbed the youth who was doing all the talking. It was bad judgment, for the whole number of black youths, looking menacing and threatening, began to visibly surge forward. The black youth whose wrist was being held by the police began to push his hand away.

"Let go mi hand, man. Go and arrest Lord Lucan for bloodclaath murder!"

The crowd roared with laughter and the policeman grew red. It also made him more violent as he tightened his grip on the youth. With the other hand he was radioing in for assistance. The crowd was becoming antagonistic to the police when the reference to Lord Lucan was made. It sunk deep in their collective minds.

"You're being arrested for preventing an officer from carrying out his duty and obstruction and for using obscene language . . ."

"Let the bloodclaath youth go!"

As the policeman tightened his grip on the youth he pulled and tugged at the policeman's hand, but the latter increased the strength of his grip even more. The youth bit his hand, suddenly and with violent rage. The policeman immediately responded by punching him straight in the face. When he did that a surge of black bodies towards the police, accompanied by punches and kicks brought about the release of both the girl and the youth. Simultaenously, police sirens were heard coming down the slight incline. The Asian man who was trying to get through the crowd met with Tubbs' right hand and Michael kicked him. When he fell some other youths stamped on him and ran off. One of the policemen was on the ground. He was red in the face and had several scratches on his arm. The other one ran back to his car. The two police cars and vans came to a sudden halt and about twenty police officers came out running. They came directly to the crowd and asked the policemen what was going on. By the time they had asked, the youths had already disappeared around the corner. About half the policemen ran off frantically, but stopped at the top of the street and returned. There were still some young black people standing around watching the proceedings. Amongst the police was a huge sergeant, well over six foot, who pulled his trousers up on his waist and said to one of the two policemen, "Right, which one of that lot was involved?" The policeman, feeling embarrassed and revengeful, pointed to two black youths who were wearing tams. The sergeant went over to them and said, "Yeh, alright, you two are fucking nicked." He was joined by about ten policemen who were taking them to the van.

"I didn't do nothin", said one of the young boys. He was about fourteen. The crowd started making a noise. "It wasn't him. That lot you're after left already, mate You got the wrong ones." This from an old white man.

"And who the fuck asked you anything? Get off the fucking street!" The sergeant waved his hand and the crowd, sensing he was going to enforce his command, simply obeyed and dispersed. The police grabbed one of the youths by the legs and arms and tossed him into the van. He was making protestations about him not being the one. He was crying. After the crowd dispersed, the police walked up and down the street as though dramatising to everybody that the law was here and any protestations would be met with forcible arrest. After another ten minutes of patrolling, they left. The Asian man had tied a handkerchief over his head and was led to a police car, probably to make a statement at the station.

They had all reached Tubbs' house. Tubbs' parents were not home. His father went to work and his mother went shopping. They crowded into Tubbs' small room with posters of Marcus Garvey, Burning Spear and Haile Selassie on the walls. They were all laughing and talking all at once. Tubbs went straight to his record box and put on Dr. Alimantado's 'Gimme Mi Gun". When the music started playing they all started rocking.

"Rockers mi want hear" one of the youths said.

"I man want a one-drop" another said.

"One drop mi bloodclaath! Just straight steppers, you hear sah!"

They laughed again and slapped each other's palms. The song was a paen against oppression, and they felt they had just taken on the symbols of white oppression in Britain – the police.

"Them bloodclaath police feel say they can come and trouble black people . . . Well, that go teach them don't fuck with me the younger generation."

"Seen, seen."

"The likkle bloodclaath gul ain't do nothin and they want arrest she. That bloodclaath Asian want a beatin. Him lying pon the daughter like she do him somethin."

"The daughter probably cuss him for him freshness, that's why he wanted to get she arrested. Fire for him bloodclaath!"

"Ey, Tubbs, the way this here youth punched down the Asian an gi him two kick I man thought is one big man that . . ."

"Yeh, the brother hard, you no see it."

"Yeh," said the youth who was nearly arrested, "we should call him Rough Black! Him is one rough youth!"

"Yeh, yeh, that sound hard to bloodclaath!"

"That sound punkish, Rasta. I man just call the I Jah Mike, you no see it?"

"But Rough Black sound hard, man, Tubbs. Like a sound system name. If the man had a sound and named Rough Black all the youth will follow him, just for the name, Rasta."

Michael had never really been involved with a gang before. He had always distanced himself from a gang, but now he felt magnatically attracted to becoming part of this group's identity. The idea of being elevated to Rough Black sound system man, appealed to him in the most basic sense of roots. He felt himself to be part of this group and without asking for recognition, they had already accepted him with open arms into their brotherhood. He was now finally replacing one family with another, a more real and attractive one. Even if the name did not fit, he felt he could grow to fit into it.

4
WORKING BLUES/BABYLON DUB ENCOUNTER PART 2

After looking at his financial situation from a variety of angles Michael decided that he had better sign on. He was earning no money and was involved with petty theft (which his friends like to call hustling). The things they stole, clothes and electrical parts, were sold pretty cheaply. Sometimes they would get £3 for a pair of jeans, £2 for a shirt, £1 for a T-shirt. The money he earned after it was divided between three or four of them wasn't very much and he really couldn't buy records or equipment for the sound he had in mind. Tubbs had spoken to him about earning some money. Tubbs himself had decided through his own reasoning that he wanted to be a carpenter, so he went and found himself a job. This meant that Michael was on his own during the day. He would then spend more of his time with his new friends and they would usually smoke ganja, hang around the shebeen, listen to records in somebody's room and end up stealing and running. Tubbs' advice to him was to sign on.

Although Tubbs' parents usually never gave Tubbs a hard time about his staying at home or having Michael there, Michael had begun to develop a feeling of self-consciousness, that Tubbs' parents were discussing him, and sometimes he read particular meaning into a glance they may have given him. He had taken a bath and dressed himself as cleanly as possible and walked over to the unemployment exchange on the Harrow Road. After queueing for nearly an hour at the Enquiries counter he was told that he did not qualify for unemployment benefits because he had never worked and was told to see the social security people. He felt like banging the desk, but restrained himself. He finally went over to the office and the sight was even worse than at unemployment. Cigarette butts were all over the floor, a couple of people were already sleeping, their heads shooting tremourously backward and forward as there was no head-rest behind the chair. A disabled white woman was complaining to the interviewer that she had asked for a visit on five previous occasions but they had never come around. Each time the woman tried to calm her down she would raise her voice to screaming level. There was an old white man walking up and down cracking jokes. Although he looked at people and made his jokes, it was as though he was really talking to himself. Then he started talking about his dog.

"Would you believe it", he said, "I was walking my dog, big helluva dog I have, believe me, and this woman, rich and snooty she was, stopped her car, big helluva car, mercury, mercedes it was, and says to me, 'Young man'. Could you imagine a woman much younger than meself calling me 'young man'? Me eyes blazing, would you believe me, I got real hot, but she never knew that see, 'Young man', she says, 'did you see my dog'. I says to her 'Are you talking to me'. She says, 'Well, I'm certainly not talking to myself, am I'? 'Well', I says, 'I ain't seen no young man around here.' Some people were laughing sheepishly but pretending they weren't listening to him. Some kept their faces glued to their newspapers, but behind the newspapers their ears were perked up. Michael looked at the man and laughed to himself, but it emerged loudly.

"The bastard didn't even blink when I said that. She just said to me, indignant like, 'Did you or did you not see my dog?' Before I could give it a thought she was back at me like a bolt: 'Answer me!' she shouted. I scratched my head I did, look, see, I ain't got no hair left, I burned it, ha ha ha ha! So I says to her, 'Lady, I ain't seen your dog, I don't know what your fucking dog looks like even if it was blue, but if you want a dog, you can fucking buy mine at a price. It will be worth your while.' I says to her. She put that big car into gear and was off like a bolt. She musta thought I was crazy, but believe me, would ya, know what I thought? I thought the ole bag was the one I read about in me paper that escaped from the lunatic bin. You know the one I mean, the one that talks about a dog. Fucking hell, I says to myself, scratching me bald patch again,

I coulda got a reward if I'd captured that ole hag. Cor! You lot are stupid if you believe that!?"

Almost everyone burst out in an uproarous laugh. The people who were sleeping got up laughing, one of them leaping into the air. A tall fat black interviewer banged her desk several times and shouted, "Will you shut up! Shut up! This is an office, not a TV show. If you want to be attended to I would advise you to pipe down. Now please shut up!' Silence fell like a cloud on the people. The old joker didn't like that and he laughed gigglyish, then said, "Cor! What a fat one she is!" Everybody started laughing again. Then a name was called out: "Metcalf, Max Metcalf, Max Metcalf." Everybody went silent again because they recognized it was money being given out. One of the sleepers jumped up and hobbled over to the wire-mesh counter. "Right here, mate, right here." The old joker laughed again, "Right mongoose this one, look at him, look at him!"

After two and a half hours Michael finally was called to the desk. The interviewer he came to was an old man. He asked Michael to sit down and began to gently ask him questions.

"What's your name?"

"Michael Blumenthal." He spelt his surname for him.

"Address?"

"45a Codrington Gardens, Harlesden."

"How much rent do you pay?"

"Well, I'm staying with a friend really, so I'm not paying any money yet, you see. But I was told that I would have to pay a fiver if I got social security."

"Yes, I see. How long have you been at that address, Mr, Blumenthine?"

"Blumenthal."

"Yes, sorry. But it's an unusual name, if you see what I mean."

"About five months really."

"What was your previous employment."

"Well, I just left school, you see."

"Yes, I see. What would you like to do then?"

"I don't know what you mean."

"Yes. Well, if you are getting social security benefits, you see, you have to show a willingness to work. Do you follow? If you don't show a willingness to work, we will have to cut you off. Do you understand?"

"Well, I never thought about it really. But, I guess, I will take any type of job."

"That's not good for a start, Mr. Blumenthine."

"Blumenthal."

"Sorry. It's that name again. We get all sorts of requests for work, but you must have some idea of what you want. Have you taken any GCEs or CSEs?"

"No. I haven't. I left before I could."

"Well, that's no good, is it? We're facing a recession in this country, jobs are scarce and only the qualified get the best jobs, and even they are having a hard time. I had a chap in here last week with a masters and he couldn't get work, so what chance do you have, ey? Anyway, the only jobs around for you, because you are unskilled, are menial ones. Working with your hands like. Just a minute, will you, I'll be back in a sec."

When the old man hobbled away, Michael stared at his hands, looked around, looked at the empty space where the interviewer was sitting and started to bite his nails. He felt nervous and jittery and a fear built up in him like a aeroplane taking off. Thoughts just flew in and out of his mind like a kite ducking in the wind. His face became red and he just kept biting his nails. The old man hobbled back with a small box and index cards in it. He sat down and began to look through it. He finally pulled one out. "This is a job as a packer, working in a factory packing cans into boxes. How does that sound?"

"Is there anything else going?"

"You don't like it by the sound of it. Yes. There are others." He looked through the box, picking up cards as he went along. He now had about five in his hand. He looked through them once more, his national health glasses resting on the bridge of his nose and his brow turned up on his forehead. "A few here. Nothing really fascinating. Then again, you don't have the qualifications, do you? There's one here, a messenger for a garment factory. You deliver goods and so on to different parts of the city, I imagine. Another here . . . operating a machine, a printing machine, it says here 'ideal opportunity for trainee', someone who has an interest in printing.

Here's another, packing and shipping. What they mean is that you pack goods up and prepare the packages or boxes or whatever with addresses, invoices, seal them and ship them. By mail or by truck, I imagine. Anything here that suits you?"

"Well, I think I'll have a go at the messenger one."

"You think so, do you?"

"Well, it sounds awright to me."

"It sounds awright, does it. Nothing to do but give it a try. See what will happen. This is no guarantee that you will get the job, but there's no harm in trying, is there. Well, here's the address. It's in the West End. I'll have to phone up for you first just to see if the job is still going, awright?"

He picked the phone up and dialled the number. He replaced the phone and picked it up again. "It's engaged," he said, "I'll have to try again. Think that's a wise choice, do you, a messenger job? I guess you like the fresh air, ey, not cooped up inside like me. Well, I guess it's as good as any. I used to live in the fresh air once, when I was in Scotland. That's a long time ago now. Let's give it a try once more, shall we?" He picked the phone up once more and dialled. "Hello, is this Steiner Fashions? Could I speak to Mrs. Appleton, please? Yes, thank you." He covered his hand over the phone and said to Michael, "I'm speaking to the woman now. Hello, Mrs.. Appleton? Yes, this is social security here. Is the messenger job still going? I have a young man here, he's just left school and nearly sixteen. I think he's very conscientious and would be quite suitable for the position really. Yes, he does know the hours, Mrs. Appleton, and he is quite willing to work. Should I send him now, did you say? Alright, then, Mrs. Appleton, I'll send him after two. Thank you. Goodbye. Looks like the job is still vacant, Michael . . . don't mind me calling you Michael, do you? Tidy up a bit, give your face a wash and off you go. Do you have money to go over there? Well, hang on a bit . . . no . . . it will take too long. Look, here's a quid. Pay me back when you get your first pay packet, awright. Alright, lad, off you go."

Michael felt a little scared and a tremour of excitement and apprehension shot through his body like lightning. He trembled. He felt good about the prospects of the job, but simultaneously he experienced a kind of fear. It came from the thought of actually working full-time. Though he had sometimes worked while at school in a sweet-shop in the afternoons and on Saturdays, he had never really worked in his life. He thought it might be a good idea to return home and fix himself up so that he could look presentable. As he followed his footsteps he felt the idea was a good one. That old man, he thought, he was alright. Nice bloke. The idea of the job, now that he had decided that he would really take it, made him feel a little more secure and less dependent and desperate. His desperation stemmed from the fact that he was dependent solely on stealing to survive and that Tubbs and his parents were too kind to him. It had been five months since he was staying with them and it made him feel childish. Because his contributions were minimal and fluctuated between when he had *hustled* a little thing. If he did not, he felt bad eating at the table. It was becoming difficult for him to even smile at Tubbs' parents. They were too understanding and kind, he thought. And when Tubbs had begun working he was giving Michael a fiver a week. Michael felt like a helpless puppy after the first three times. He was certain that Tubbs was giving out of the kindness of his heart and because he wanted to, but Michael could not avoid feeling belittled. But this job, he thought, would really solve his embarrassing situation . . .

Mrs. Appleton was a tall, brown-haired, fattish woman. She didn't speak with any kind of particular kindness, but with a clipped, to-the-point, business accent. This threw Michael off somewhat, but he was sufficiently quiet, and responsive only when she asked a direct question, that she hired him straight away. She explained how the office worked, that they were a garment distributor, that no actual sewing was conducted on their premises, but that their goods were sometimes delivered by hand to some customers. That money in the form of cheques were sometimes collected and that he would have to demonstrate an ability to be trusted before he could handle that aspect of the business. She made sure to tell him that if deliveries were slack that some appropriate work would have to be found for him to do in the office, like cleaning. She watched his face intently to observe his response when she said that, but Michael only nodded and said, "Alright." She figured that from the demeanour and behaviour of this boy, that she had found the right person. Before she had sent him off with a delivery, she confirmed that she would call social security to let them know that he had gotten the job.

As he jumped on the train he had begun to relive some of the times he had with the brethren he had accepted as friends after he had kicked the Asian man. He was almost caught the second time. The first was the incident in the Boots store when he was actually arrested and charged. About three of them had gone to a house which Nose (that's what they called him because his nose was enormous) was casing for a couple weeks. Nose had worked out that the small two-storey house was occupied by a man he presumed to be homosexual. The man usually went away for the weekend and there was no one there to disrupt their plans. Nose used a knife to get the lock opened. Stabber followed him in, while Michael stood outside to keep watch. In three minutes Nose and Stabber ran out of the house with a stereo and tape recorder in their hands, followed by a white youth in his pyjamas. The white youth stopped at the door and re-entered the house. There was a squad car coming around the corner. Nose and Stabber were already out of sight. Michael panicked when he saw the police and started to run. They saw him, caught up with him, snatched him by the collar, pushed him against a wall and searched him.

"Got something to run away from, mate?"

"Can't you speak?" The shorter one asked.

"What you running from then, John?"

"Nicked something and tossed it away, did ya?"

"No!"

"So you can talk, eh?"

"Come on, John, you might as well tell us the story or you might have to spend a couple of days in the nick. Would like that, would ya?"

"Look, I saw two guys running down the street and when I saw you, I thought you were after them and might nick me, see. I panicked and ran, that's all."

"That's all, is it?"

"Yeh."

"What about your mates, what were they running from, ey? Training for the olympics, were they, I know you blackies are good at athletics and sport . . ."

"Look, I don't even know them. Straight up, officer, I don't."

"That's coming from the heart, is it, John?"

"I'm telling ya the truth. Straight up.Lots of my friends tell me how the police do them over like, so I got scared and ran, that's all."

"What's your name then, and don't give me no aliases."

"Aliases! Look, my name is Michael Blumenthal."

"Michael Blumenthal, eh?"

"Yeh, that's right."

"Ere, you hear that. His name is Michael Blumenthal!"

"He must be a fucking black Jew!"

"Well, if your name is Michael Blumenthal, mine is Ojonju! Ha ha ha ha!"

"What's so funny, then? That's my name; it is!"

"What's your address then? You live in Hampstead, do you? Ha ha ha ha!"

"Nah, I live in Harlesden. 45a Codrington Gardens, NW10."

"We're taking ya in, mate."

"What for?"

"What for?" asked the shorter one. "We don't know. Do you know, mate?" The other cop shook his head. "Well, let's start with SUS. Come on, let's go."

When they took him into the station they made him empty his pockets out on to the desk, removed his tam and the sergeant showed great hostility to him. He had to answer all the questions he was already asked. But this time they asked country of birth. He answered Britain and the sergeant laughed and looked up at him, then made a face. He had a bangle on his right wrist and they told him to remove it. He was kept in the station for three hours while they checked his address and probably tried to hook up with the burgled house and his presence in the area. He was then let out. All the time he was in there, he felt a tightening knot in his stomach and his arse kept opening and closing. His chest was pounding with fear as the police came to look through the small peep-through at him, almost every half hour. They didn't press any charges, but told him if they found him running in the street next time they would lose his arse in jail. When they gave him his tam, there was a hole in it. He cussed under his breath and walked away.

In the cell next to him he could hear voices raised and another stammering and shouting. At the back of his cell, on the floor, there was an air vent. He walked over and knelt down, putting his ears to it. It was obvious from the questioning, the impatience and the heavy thuds, that a man (from the accent it sounded Irish) was being beaten up. He heard the police ask, "So where did you hide it, ey?" The man stammered, making sobbing sounds, and a heavy thud echoed, the man groaning and shouting, "You bastards!" More heavy thuds followed, and the man sounded like he was spitting. Michael didn't want to hear any more, the sounds were creating fear and horror in him, and he was praying to God that they did not hit him. One of the police had slapped his head in the car on his way to the station, because he did not answer a question readily enough and because they thought he was involved. His head had bobbed forward and he had felt slightly giddy. They threatened him, but he was not touched up.

He had nearly missed his stop as the doors were about to close, but he quickly recognised Liverpool Street. He had been to this station once or twice before, and it always brought to his mind the pictures he had seen in school of old England, England of the late 19th century, early 20th century. He had found something romantic and intimate about these pictures. It was as though there was a hidden humanity, a hidden love that once sparked in the heart of this cold, alienated and racist country. It was as though a world existed within it that he felt he could reach into and communicate. He felt as though as the country itself modernised, a heart within it became corrupted and stank. The transformation of the face of the country was the transformation of the country's soul. But, he countered, if that was so, why were there slaves? The soul-heart was always stink and corrupted, he finally concluded. His mind must have invented meaning into simple pictures. Blood-claath Babylon system still! a sudden anger unfolded in his brain, and he ran up the escalator, paid fifteen pence, keeping the excess change for himself.

He asked the news vendour for directions, but the man ignored him for two minutes, selling his papers to clients, and when he did turn to him, it was with a cold and hostile stare. "What do you want?" Michael hesitated for a moment, then asked the question, and the man did not make a verbal reply, but only pointed across the road and sold another newspaper, his face turning away almost immediately. Michael crossed the street, walked down the side street where people were looking for bargains at the back-street shops. He kept walking, feeling his direction without asking any questions. He turned into another side street where a pub stood at the corner, walked two more streets down and saw the street that he wanted. He walked into it and came to a small dirty shop front, MAGGIE'S FASHIONS. Inside the small congested room was unpainted, or rather, the paint had faded twenty years ago, and there were stacks of children's clothes piled one on top of the other, all over the shop. Almost like a book or a film, a woman emerged with horn-rimmed glasses with a black string attached and around her head, the glasses resting on the bridge of her nose. She looked like she ate horses for dinner. She pushed the glasses up on her forehead, while Michael was unloading the small box onto a bigger box on the floor, but before he could place it, the woman said, "Ahahahah, no, give it to me. New boy, are you?" He did not answer, and she continued opening the box, picking up an envelope, read the contents, looked at him and said, "Just wait one minute, young man." Her massive flesh in a loose-fitting black dress moved to the back of the shop and returned with a reasonably sized box. "That's for you, young man. Now there's a note in there for Mrs Appleton. Thank you." Michael picked up the box and walked slowly out of the shop, stunned by the whole proceedings. It happened so quickly, the unfriendly acknowledgement of his presence, the taking and returning of boxes, and the quick dismissal. He was almost dreaming while walking back to the station, when it entered his mind that he ought to walk around the area. He discovered that there were different sides to this seemingly impoverished area. He went down a one-way street and was surprised to find that it led to an open roundabout with a well-kept square within it, surrounded by elegantly decorated buildings. He stood on the pavement admiring this, then walked on to the right exit where a cafe was, with people eating and drinking and talking with business-like faces. Two buildings down there was an amusement arcade. He stood holding the box in his arms, contemplating whether he should go in. The people inside were young, and he figured they might well be school kids. He went in and put a ten pence piece into a slot machine. There was writing on the machine that explained the game, and before he could start, a young white guy came up to him.

"It's easy, mate", the boy said. "Let me show you." The young guy seemed to be very good, because he had gotten all his shots right and about ten ten-pence pieces came out of the machine. Michael picked them up, astounded and grinning and offered the guy half, but he waved it away, "Nah, mate, it's yours, you keep it." Michael was insisting , but the guy refused, "Go on, you have a go. It's easy." Michael played the game, aiming at the target and firing, but fifty pence later he gave up. "You'll soon get the hang of it," the white guy said. "Working round here, are ya? I ain't seen your face before, My name's Ronald, everyone calls me Ron, what's yours, mate? Michael? That's alright. What's in a bleeding name. Call me Ron. I work around here meself, sort of an office boy like, you know, do a bit of everything. It pays me rent, what do I care. I bet the horses, sometimes I win, sometimes I lose, know what I mean? Keeps me going. Then there's a little hustling on the side. What line are you in? Clothes? That's all right. I'm in the stationery business. I get me orders from round where I live, take them, sell them, sometimes I make thirty nickers a week. Yeah, it's awright. Clothes is alright though, If you got the contacts you can do well on that. It takes time, you gotta build it up slowly. Took me a couple of years to work myself up to what I'm doing now. I don't save a penny though. Take me girl out, buy me mum and me dad some nice things. Now and again, though, when I have the change like. They awright. They know the scheme like. Me dad said just as long as I'm not caught. With a job like this, who is ever?"

Mrs. Appleton was beginning to manifest a slackening of her emotional distance and detachment from Michael. She was beginning to show some degree of trust and faith in him; even though Michael felt that he was killing time when he delivered packages and letters, Mrs. Appleton measured the length of time he stayed on a particular job in comparison with previous employees. She felt that Michael's performance was desirous of some sort of reward, and she demonstrated this by allowing him to receive small cheques, and she would take him into the office when work was slack and show him the methods used for filing. Michael made very few errors and when Mrs. Appleton called for the file on a client, moaning about the length of their debt, Michael knew almost immediately where to get it. He also began to decipher the type of voice-tone she would employ when talking about a particular client. Those who paid well, were always talked about flowingly, and she had a kind of contempt for those who were late. He began to instinctively understand the type of mood she was in by the manner of her walk or by the fixation of her pout. He knew when to make himself invisible and what to do when she placed her head in her hands – he would prepare a cup of black coffee for her and she would smile affectionately, sipping elegantly, her headache or frustration almost magically disappearing.

The other women in the office knew that Mrs. Appleton liked Michael, and would similarly display some kind of affection for him. Since Mrs. Appleton was in the enviable position of being the chief executive (she was the sister of the boss' wife), the other office staff knew what trends to follow once exemplified by Mrs. Appleton. Consequently, Michael was always being given, rather, offered, sweets and chocolates (but he almost never accepted; if he did, it was only to please and then threw them away). They would also ask him to buy something from the shop: it could be a sandwich, fish & chips, or some edible thing. Sometimes they would tell him to buy something for himself which he almost never did, keeping the money instead. The responsibility he had begun to accept, only after four months, was beyond his comprehension. Now when he came into the office and Mrs. Appleton wasn't there, he would go through the papers on her desk and take out the orders that he felt needed filling. If the decision was a little too much for him, he would consult with Mrs. Bromberg, a fiftyish, greying Jewish lady who ate kosher food, and did not share the enthusiasm for him as the others, i.e., she did not display emotional empathy or attempt to imitate Mrs. Appleton's behaviour towards him. Rather, she was an independent woman with what seemed to Michael, to be some degree of *class* and pedigree. She treated him with business-like calmness, but without any undue disregard for his personality. Of all the women who worked there, she seemed to be the least likely to be touched in a working relationship by anybody. She seemed the type of woman who made personal friends outside the environment of the office.

Michael was not surprised when he first came upon Mrs. Appleton's husband, a small, balding man with a beard and moustache. He would come round the office once in a while, and never displayed any great friendliness for the other staff. He usually said the time of day and asked the state of their health and went straight to his wife. Once he asked Michael to go into his car, a two-year old Vauxhall, and bring a box that was in the back seat. Because the car was locked, he had to unlock the front door, and when he did he saw the locker was not locked, and tried it, he was amazed to see a roll of £20 and £10 notes stacked in an envelope. His first instinctual response was to take some, but he thought Mrs. Appleton had deliberately put her husband up to it and was testing his honesty. The next day Mrs. Appleton made him keep a pound that he brought back from a job. He felt then that it was in fact a deliberate ploy.

There was no personal fulfilment in the job. It only proved that he could be self-reliant if he wanted to, that he could hold down a job and support himself. There was no difference in Tubbs' parents' attitude to him. They did not laud him with praise for getting and keeping a job, and when, after the first week, he offered them money, they refused, saying that it was only his first week and that he should buy some necessary things for himself first. For a whole month he bought shirts, jeans, a pair of shoes, underpants, and other small necessary things. At the end of the first month he had given them £15 out of a take-home salary of £29 a week. They were putting up a fight, but he explained that they deserved it and that he appreciated their support. The next week he gave them £10 and brought home a plant for Tubbs' mother. She was very much moved by this and that night she cooked a special meal which they all sat down and ate with relish. Michael was glad that they saw him as a son or a nephew and felt completely integrated into this family fabric.

In spite of all the warmth and friendliness and love, he felt that the room was too small for both himself and Tubbs. They had become increasingly close and he sometimes thought how is it that two people, not being related, could strike up a friendship like they were born brothers. But the thought of remaining a boarder and sharing Tubbs' room for much longer struck a discordant chord in him. Tubbs sometimes brought his girl friend to the house at weird hours. It could be two in the morning or twelve in the day. Sometimes Michael would be sleeping, resting or reading, a habit that he became increasingly attached to, and he would have to move out to the livingroom or leave the house completely. Although Tubbs tried to reassure him that it was alright, he felt that he was an interloper in a situation that demanded intimacy and privacy. Even though a lot of his friends would have stayed there and pretended to be asleep, listening to sexual moanings and groanings, Michael could not stand that type of situation. In fact, the idea disgusted him.

What had started him off on reading was the fact that he had been to a local community centre when he was in trouble with the law, and they had a library downstairs where he was given his conference with one of the legal consultants and purely through curiosity, while waiting for the man to come from upstairs, he looked through the hundreds of books on the shelf and saw a lot of books on African history and culture. A huge book called *VANISHING AFRICA* intrigued him, because it carried a great number of pictures about Africans from East Africa, and a lot of them wore locks. He started reading the writing and understood that locks was a symbol of warriorship among the young adults and that they were shaved by their mothers when moving into adulthood. That first bit of information wetted his curiosity to understand more about African culture and history and how it related to what he was beginning to himself practise. He had also seen some African films about people living in the rural communities and was amazed with the dance-movements of these people, and how absolutely similar their dancing was to their own.

From that point on he started buying cheap paperback books about African culture and history and read and discussed them with Tubbs. Tubbs also showed some interest, but he didn't seem to have the emotional zeal that Michael experienced deep within him.

The street was filled with people looking for bargains: antiques (and those that were faked), Mexican rugs and blankets, African sculpture, second hand clothes, cookers, fridges, furniture, etc., anything that was saleable. The market people had regular customers and when Michael stopped at a stall he could pick up snatches of conversation. There was an Asian man selling Indian oils, soap, incense and stainless steel cutlery. An old Jamaican woman was having an exchange with him, "How much I owe you now?" "Oh forget it", he said, "see me next week." She laughed, "I don't like to owe people much, you know. Let me settle meh debts with you now." "Oh, pay me next week, love." "You have that nice Indian soap? It nice, you know". She turned to her old friend. "He sell some nice soap. You know someting, Mattie, is meh cousin Isabel who tell me bout this, you know. And ever since I been buying from this man. But he too cheat!" She laughed. The man was laughing too, selling somebody else while continuing his conversation with the old woman. The man's son was also selling. "You calling me cheat? Nah nah. I'm a fair man. Go on, have it until next week. Look, I have some nice soap for you, just like that . . .". "You not a cheat love, you're a nice man. I was only joking. He's a nice man, Mattie. I always buy from him, you know". "You want it?" he asked, giving somebody some change. "Is the same one like last week, you say?" "Yes," he said, "It's the same one. Jasmine. Look, look, I also have some rose. Smell it, nice, eh?" He pushed it to her nose and she passed it to Mattie to smell. A white girl was taking photographs of them as they talked. Michael turned his face away. "Yes, it nice, but I like the jasmine better. Gimme the jasmine." He picked up one of the soaps and was passing it to her, when she said, "No, I better have two. I send them to Jamaica, you know. My sister Gladys always write and ask me for this soap, and she say how much it bring relief to her rheumatism." He passed the two soaps to her, then picked up one of the rose. "Why don't you try this as well." He smelled it, smiled, and passed it to her. She laughed, pushing his hand back away from her. He smelled it again and smiled. "This man too smart, ey. I tell him I don't want no more soap, but he still selling me. Awright, gimme the dam soap, you too smart." He passed her two, still smiling. "You want any incense? Look, I have some nice coconut. Smell it. Nice, eh? Take one and try it". She laughed again and took it to her nose. "You too dam smart!" "That's free. That one is free. You can have that. It's a present. Take it, take it." She laughed, covering her mouth and looking at Mattie. Mattie's face was non-plussed, she just kept looking at the Asian man. "No, I ain't taking the dam ting. I like to pay for everting I buy." He still insisted that it was free, she insisting that she would pay, then to settle the argument he said, "Pay me next week, pay me next week", just so that she would accept it without knowing that he wasn't going to charge her. Michael walked on.

About four stalls up, Michael came to some Rasta brethren selling newspapers, books, tams, caps, badges with Selassie 1 picture on them, and other Rasta paraphernalia. A brethren in battle fatigues had a stack of newspapers in his hand and shouting, "Grass-roots!" Two white girls and a white man in horn-rimmed glasses bought some from the brethren. Michael was about to pass him, when he shouted again. Michael bought one and was about to move on when another brethren asked him, "Buy a Selassie badge nuh, bredder? It only 50 pence. Support I & I." Michael bought one, and smiled and kept on walking. On the other side of the street there was a little crowd gathered. When he went to see what was happening, he saw several things: there was an old Italian woman sitting on a chair, playing an Italian record and singing to the record. There was nobody watching her. There was a cleanly dressed black man with a loud-hailer in his hand, talking about Christ and the impending doom. The crowd was around a white guy playing an electric guitar, the sound emerging from it was very messy, but the mostly white crowd seemed to like it. A girl was accompanying him on tambourine and vocals. It was a kind of Blues. Michael didn't know anything about the Blues, but he knew it was Black Man music, and he sucked his teeth. The girl was feigning emotion, allowing her forehead to crease and closing her eyes. Michael felt like spitting on her or throwing a stone, but he walked on up the street.

In front of the community organization there was a brother selling Afrikan sculpture, but it was of the East Afrikan tourist variety. He stood looking at them, thinking that a piece would look nice in his room. He wanted something that would reflect his spirit. There were animals, women with babies on their backs, men, etc., but the one that attracted him was a warrior standing erectly with a staff in his hand. He had long locks down to his shoulders and the expression on his face was one of serenity, consciousness andpower.

He stood looking intently at the object, seeing the almost majestic power that the piece of wood exuded, enclosed in its still worlds of dreams. "I man will tek that piece dey, bredder". The young brother who sold the sculpture smiled broadly, Reggae music blasting from his portable cassette, "Nice nice. That is £5.50". Michael peeled a £5 note from his wallet and gave it to him, "Dat cool"? The brother hesitated, the smile momentarily disappearing, then just as suddenly reappearing with a flash, "Yeh yeh. That cool, man".

When he looked down the street where the white blues singers were, he saw two policemen holding a white man with a bike. He must have tried to ride down the one-way street, Michael thought. The man was standing with the bike in one arm and the two policemen standing on each side of him holding an arm. As Michael pushed open the door, the smell of brandy greeted him, creating instantaneous nausea. The fresh air flew in and gave him an aromatic reawakening. There were at least twelve men in varrying ages from 21 to 50 sitting or standing around talking. Some were shouting, laughing and heatedly discussing. The brother who he recognized as Jordan, in charge of the centre, was stating something . . .

Jordan

. . . And what worries me is that inspite of whatever political persuasion, whatever political view they might hold . . . Alright, you've come from a middle-class . . . or not even middle-class, privileged, really . . . that kind of background, and you come here and you find that this society doesn't recognize, really, what class you may have belonged to . . . It's just a race thing . . . Whether you black, brown-skinned, light-skinned, Indian or what, its just a race thing. And you discover that and move to Black Power, Socialism or whatever! and they still have this very strong contempt for the working-class black man . . .

Vidal

(Caribbean Indian barrister)

What you don't realise (drunkenly) is that the classes must be kept apart, man! It's we (slapping his chest), we professionals who you have to come to for help, man!

Jordan
O fuck, man, Vide, get offa that humour thing, man. (To someone else) Do you understand what I', saying, man?

Ralph
(Dreadlocked)
You are quite right, of course, but the dimension of the Caribbean bourgeoisie is that his training had begun at home! He had been trained to despise himself since a child, you must remember, and coming here is, sort of, a fulfilment of an often held, long held dream. The dream of coming here, rather than diminishing his bourgeois aspirations, of course, increased it, escalated it. Racism is real, of course, but he transcends it and makes up for it by further imitating and inculcating in his person the very forms of white European contempt and oppression that he has experienced, that he has known existed. But that European contempt is reinforced with a very heavy class bias, you see my point? Class! Style, symbols that he is accustomed to from his middle-class Caribbean up-bringing. Thus he perpetuates his bourgeois prejudices by his imitation of the bourgeois life-style that he enjoys at pain! And, of course, the Caribbean man, this black discarded man, reminds him, indelibly, of himself!

Vidal
Stop all the bullshit sociological jargon and pass the bottle, man! I want a drink!

Jordan
Cool it, man, just cool it. (He looks disappointed and frustrated)

Vidal
I need a drink, man! (He struggles with the bottle from a big fat black man, both of them laughing boisterously. Another dreadlocked brother talking at the other desk, passes his hand over his head, expresses great anger and shouts; "Shut up, please! You'll just have to be quiet!")

Thank you, Max. (He pours the drink and sips it) You are making a point, Jordan, but you are taking it too bloody far! The professional black man does have prejudices, middle-class ones if you will, but you must admit that he makes a considerable contribution to the scheme of things.

Jordan
I'm not talking about the quality of his contributions, man. I'm talking about something else. You have a professional black person, be he man or woman, and there is something that happens inside that person's head the minute they realise that they are different from the ordinary working man. They begin to display a kind of . . . no, not a kind of, but contempt, pure and simple. And something should be done about that really. OK, OK . . .

Max
Look, I'm getting rather bored with this conversation. Let's talk about something else, rather than stick with this philoso . . . philosophising. Look how Williams has placed the entire Compact organization in jeopardy by becoming involved with fucking a 13 year old girl. That's much more important to discuss, rather than waste our time talking about middle-class professionals! I happen to be middle class, so what? (He laughed and Jordan roared, joined by everybody)

Jordan
OK, OK, Max . . . Let's hear what you have to say.

Max
To be frank, putting all bullshit aside, right, I think that all this talk about professional middle-class is fine, but it's not taking us anywhere. For one thing the black middle-class is just what they are – middle-class, and we can rant and rave for the next five years, its still not going to change their attitude.

Jordan
O come off that, man, come off that!

Max
Its true . . .

Jordan
Aaaaaahhhhhh, get off that shit!

Max
Now, let's not dwell (fixing his shades and pointing) on that. We have ideological differences, if you will, but . . .

Jordan
Nice one, Max! (Laughter all round, handclaps)

Max
But the point is we have to work together. Now the point I was making is this: a serious aberration took place right on Compact's doorstep, as it were, and it was taken lightly by the staff and the management committee.

Jordan
It wasn't taken lightly, Max. You're not justified in saying that really. The management committee took certain steps . . .

Max
But those steps were too late. Now, I had put a motion to the committee that William, no matter that he's my friend and we've worked together before, that William ought to be banned for life from entering Compact's premises. (Jordan attempts to butt in). Wait a minute, wait a minute, I haven't finished yet. Now, the day that William brought that hi-fi set, stolen property, and placed it in Compact's premises, and came into Compact at any hour of the day or night (he fixed his shades again) and God knows what he was getting up to, and both myself and Robert brought it to the management committee's attention and even went so far to recommend certain measures that were objected to by certain members of the management committee . . .

Jordan
It's me, why yuh don't say it's me? Of course I objected. It was my right to voice an opinion and I still think that I was right. I mean the brother was in jail, we were his friends, we were the only rassclath people he knew. It was our righteous raasclath duty to provide for the brother . . .

Max
It was our duty to provide, but not with our eyes closed. It is one thing for a man to be my friend on a personal level, but when it comes to business there should be and is a difference . . .

Jordan
No, I can't let you get away with that bloodclath skank, man! No, no, I protest! (Laughter).

Max
It is a position of responsibility that we are defending. If we allow our friendship with certain individuals to intervene in our working relationship with other people, all you will do is put everybody in jeopardy. I mean friend is friend, and work is work. The management committee, and you in particular, Jordan, erred. It was a serious mistake to have William fucking around the house.

Jordan
No, no, no. Let's get this in perspective. William had been among us, just as you are now, right, resting with us and functioning reasonably efficiently. No one can doubt that! So you really can't isolate this incident as though it didn't have a history. The brother went to jail, came out, and continued checking us out. Now, no one had an inkling that he was bringing stolen property into Compact. I mean no one would suspect that . . .

Max
O rubbish! Both myself and Robert had stated quite clearly to the management committee that when William was asked whose hi-fi equipment it was, he did not give a satisfactory answer. He didn't just sneak the equipment in, you know, but he took a taxi, a

taxi, and had the audacity to ask Robert to help him unload the stuff. Now if that ain't arrogance, I don't know what is! Now, you can't say to me at this hour (looking at his watch) that those things didn't happen, that the management committee wasn't forewarned. And when the police came around there making enquiries about William . . . can you imagine that? . . . William gave not only the telephone number, but the address of Compact to the police! Now, that is the height of irresponsibility! (He jumped out of his chair, the chair fell over, and he banged the desk, fixing his shades once more).

Vidal

The man is right, man! He should have been kicked out and thrown out the fucking door, man! (Laughter) How can you have such a scondrel as a friend, hhhmmm, Jordan? Is it because you are also a damned scondrel? (Laughter) No (Seriously), I support the view as so articulately propounded by my colleague, Max. There's no getting away from it, the management committee acted irresponsibly. Now it's all over the blasted newspapers and Compact's name gets even more tarnished, it is already in dire straights, and the authorities, naturally, it is to be expected of them, can bring about a great deal of scandal if they so please, i.e., if they are so inclined.

Max

Thank you, Vidal. Now I must be going. (He rises, fixes his glasses and begins to walk away)

Jordan

Now that you've said your piece, you're splitting, eh? Yuh right, yes, yuh right.

Max

No. It's not that. I have a previous appointment. (Looking at his watch). Anyway, next week, next week. And Jordan! Don't buy no cheap brandy, eh! (Laughter. Michael was observing the whole scene with a kind of awe and incredulity. Two middle-aged women were waiting to be served by the lawyers and they were both laughing and shaking their heads).

Vidal
Yes. Take care, man. See you. (Back to his drink)

The dreadlocksed brother who was sitting at the desk at the far end was finished talking to his client. He got up and walked over to where the brandy was. He looked around, and Jordan gave him his own glass, pouring some more brandy and adding coke. "Thank you,
Mr. Jordan." He sipped the drink and looked around him. He noticed the two middle-aged ladies and addressed them, "Are you ladies being served?" One answered, "Well, I was waiting for Mr. Tutu, since he knows about it." The brother sipped his drink, "I see. Is it about the Council's compulsory purchase of your house?" The woman nodded her head. "I believe Mr. Tutu is seeing a client downstairs. Let me check for you". Jordan confirmed that he was seeing somebody, but the brother said he would find out how soon he would be ready. He skipped down the stairs, leaving his drink on the desk.

Michael was thinking whether he had picked the right time to check out the books. He was beginning to feel a little uneasy when he saw Robert Johnson come in with a blue army coat and a red scarf, with a peaked black cap on. Vidal was the first to greet, "The Black community's imminent solicitor!" Robert laughed and replied, "The United Kingdom's imminent Queen's Counsel or is it recently appointed judge"? They both laughed simultaneously, joined in by the others. There was a perceptible change in the expression of Vidal: his brows creased and a stern look magically appeared. It was as though the repartee had produced an emotional response that reflected the thinking of his heart. "Not quite yet", he smiled. "But, one lives and hopes". Jordan burst out with heavy laughter, completely understanding the total context of the exchange.

When the noise level died, Robert recognized Michael and greeted him. "How's the man? Things under control"? Michael nodded. "Yeah. I'm working now, you know. And I just came down here to look through the books, you know."

"You chose a bad day for that. Saturdays is usually lawyers".

"I see that now, but I didn't know".

"Sometimes the lawyers leave early. If that happens today, you can probably browse for an hour or so. Ask this brother, Jordan, or the brother with the locks, Owusu. In fact Owusu could give you some sound advice on what books to read. That's his thing."

"Yeah, I did come in here before about the law thing and did check the books out and find them interesting like. So I just came down to check them out, you know. See if I could learn something. But I man could always come back a next day, you know".

Owusu returned from downstairs, told the women that Mr. Tutu would be another ten minutes, and returned to his drink. Robert approached him, asking whether Michael could use the library and suggested it may be possible if the lawyers left early. Owusu was doubtful, but on the basis of their friendship, agreed to do it. When Robert returned to tell Michael it would be OK, Michael thanked him and said that he would return later. He walked out of the office feeling somewhat regenerated. He walked in the direction of Goldborne Road, looking at various items with restive interest, and tightly clutching the sculpture in his hands. When he reached to the top of the street, he stood in a corner, unwrapped it and gazed at it again. He wrapped it back up and kept on walking and looking at objects. He did not know where his feet were leading him, but he already knew that he was not returning to the Centre today. As he walked he was attracted to some beautiful sisters, either Roots or made-up, and he would follow their walk down the street with his eyes, or stood watching as they bought something. One young woman was very striking. She wore a black net scarf around her head and wrapped around her shoulders, and her eyes were shaped with some very black stuff that looked like coal. She was short and black and her eyes were dramatic and hypnotic. He kept thinking of her as his feet led him up Ladbroke Grove . . .

Inside, the temperature had risen to about 90 degrees and the flock had now packed the two rooms out, ramming each other against pure sweated flesh, the smell of marijuana, beer, whisky and rum. This was an abandoned building, some lazy landlord had left it in total disrepair to rot and wait for demolition, or maybe it was already sold to the Council and now awaiting to be destroyed by bulldozers to be replaced by what a friend described as "coffin boxes", an array of six or eight storey buildings with small rooms built to contain families of varying sizes. This building was here, at the back of a *breaker*, those con men who lived off old and disfigured cars, to sell their various parts: wheels, lights, steering wheel, engine, gear box, etc. It was a street already demolished. This building was the sole one standing. On the skyline could be seen a number of put up Council houses, straddling the air like some usurped demon of vengeance. It was an ugly sight.

The people inside the building, some of them already occupants of buildings like the one that stretched the horizon, were oblivious of their marooned surroundings. The power of the sound system had transported their dead souls to a place full of life and beautiful things. Some were on the dole, others worked hard at various jobs and escaped from their daily hell by escaping into a world that was already emotionally familiar. It was not unusual for a place like this to have white girls, either prostitutes or girls married to or living with a black man, who fastened onto the music and their men like they had always belonged there. *The Messiah* was the resident sound, he had been here since this place was captured at least a year ago and he had entertained his clients with a music whose depth touched the depth of their souls, put fire into emotions, and light into dead red eyes . . . His music, he liked to proclaim, was "historical . . .. Black Man Music . . . where he came from . . . and telling you where he going . . . This sound ain got no national boundaries . . . Jah say destroy the bloodclaath passbook! . . . Is just bloodclaath Black Music Sound . . ."

The predominant experience was Reggae, but *The Messiah* was himself from Trinidad and, recognizing the dominance of the Jamaican presence and experience in England, felt that the total Black experience should be reflected and expressed: thus Calypso (in its new form Soca), Soul/Funk and Afrikan music was sporadically played, giving the flock a sense of newness and cultural identity. The Messiah did not affect a great number of people, but those he affected were deeply moved. Rastas were not his primary regulars, but another type of blackman, with a different type of complexity and defiance, and who saw his existence as one long unbroken and continuous struggle. He could not take the *youth* experience of total Reggae, because that was not his background and up-bringing, and could more easily identify with the cross-cultural musical experiences that *The Messiah* was projecting.

When a group of Rastas entered and heard this other type of Black experience they usually cussed and made fun of *The Messiah*, but when they got into the depths of the musical portrayal, some felt some emotional and cultural kinship. Michael rested in the corner of the room watching Tubbs rubup with his daughter. They danced magnetically, as though glued together by some invisible hand or act . . . Michael had a spliff that was passed to him by Nose who has just returned to the streets having served a three-month sentence. Nose told him the story that he had already heard. 'I man hate advantage! Yeah, man! That is one bloodclath ting I man can't stand, is advantage. I man sight up two youths fighting, one a bald-head, di other yout a rasta. Rough Black, you shoulda see how dis soulhead dress up. Him a wear leather pants and ting, leather blood-clath jacket, earring in him ear like him a pop star. And dis blood-clath ol black man come an defend di soulhead. I man hate advantage, and a rasta too. So I man give the bloodclath one butt inna him head and split him forehead. Di man bleed like a blood-clath pig; him a fall to di ground and bawl for him bloodclath life. When di bloodclath soulhead see dis him tek off for him life, rasta! Yes, mahn. Him just tek off like a bloodclath concorde. But guess what? Dis bloodclath born-again christian ole woman who know I from a yout went to inform on di I. White people was dey, mi bredder, and dem doh say nothin, yet dis bloodclath christian woman went and tell the Babylon dem. Inform on I! They came to I gates, but I man already get di message that dem dey bout, so I man just treks. But wha? Dem a keep a eye out for I, seen? So each time I man a trek is just bloodclath Babylon about. Rasta, mi tell you, I was feeling good, walking down di road, irie, you know, and two Babylon just a tek off behind I. I man just ups and dust! I trek down di mews and guess wha – behind me the foot soldiers and in front I the Babylon inna black maria. I man just stop. I seh to meself, bwoy, is better I man just tek di blows like a man instead of dem add on extra charges on I. So dem rough me up to prove dem is the boss, spread mi legs open, search I, put I hands behind I back and handcuff I. When I reach di station dem lay some blows on I, but I cool still. Dem tink dem have me, but I man check for di ILEA worker, what him name dey, and him come to court and say a few words. Dem fine I and put I on a suspended sentence, but wha? I man doh check for dem tings dey. I man doh pay nothin, I! I man serve di three months rather than pay dem bloodclath fine! For who? For some baldhead, no I! Even di ILEA man offer to pay I fine, but I man refuse dat, mahn. I serve two months and dem let I off. Nah must mahn!' Michael already had known the story, and he also knew that the ILEA official had the highest respect for him because Nose had the respect and attention of the youths. But more importantly, the ILEA man feared Nose because he was fearless and was not cowed by violence upon him or jail.

Stabber was chatting up a sister with straightened hair, a fat body and face and looked about 27. She looked battered and bruised and had definitely, he thought, seen better days. But Stabber found her sexually appealing because both her thighs and breasts were huge. He gave her a spliff and she smoked it. After about five minutes she allowed herself to be placed against the wall where Stabber grinded against her. The sensations she felt reminded her of her youth. She was only 20. Stabber was excited by the contours of this girl and knew that he must have her. Nose was nudging Michael and laughing. He turned to the wall, placed his hands on his face and laughed into them. When Michael passed the spliff back to him, he inhaled and coughed in his hands, actually spitting saliva. But his laughter was contained within himself, except for a few sobs that escaped.

"This here a bloodclaath Roots music! Anyone coming on here for the first night, welcomed to the shebeen. This here is *THE MESSIASH*, appointed by the one and only ever loving JAH to lighten the burden of your load, to bring light to places of darkness, and to heal the sick, and put fire on the bloodclaath WICKED! Black man rise and a Babylon fall! Rise to the ridim and get rid of de chicken! Black man a bawl and a Babylon fall! Music of culture, music of history, music of we bloodclaath roots! Leggo Babylon ways . . . Come to de altar where de black man doe falter! . . ." He kept wailing into the mike like a man appointed to the task of Redemption, his frail body, even in the dark amber light through which a red bulb over the turntable shone, was in stilled motion:

the little action that it created brought to mind a stiffening, heightening emotion. Like the feeling of words and music welled, nay, swelled up in him, expanding his mental state and reverberating through his body in economic small movements. His head swayed back and forth, side to side, and the flock on the floor in unison, in oneness with him and the music and the spirit. JAH! was an absolute and irrevocable communicant, speaking directly through the magnetism and power of the music and *The Messiah* to the flock, in possession of a one-mind/Spirit and the throbbing pulse in the temples and heads of the flock, even the white ones, created an ecstacy of beingness, being there, to an all Powerful/ all-pervasive message . . .

The Messiah continued his sermon and abruptly broke off. A white guy with a red, gold and green tam was jumping up and down, face in perpetual grin, waving a green handkerchief, and relentlessly puffing at a spliff. Nose looked contemptuously at the guy, gravitated closely to him, dancing, and pushed him "accidentally" hard against the wall. The blow stunned him for a minute, but he was back on the floor continuing his testimony. Michael laughed almost raucously, tapping his face. Nose walked back over to Michael, "That bloodclaath bredder dey, him doan learn nothin. I man shoulda thump him bloodclaath down . . . Still, is Jah works. Look at the punky bombaclaath. Him don't even feel the music, but him say him a dance! . . ." Stabber still had the girl against the wall and she now had both arms around his shoulders and her head on his chest. Stabber's eyes were transfixed somewhere between space and the room. He was looking open-eyed, but seeing nothing. Nose kept grinning as he looked at Stabber throw his waist like fire-darts at the girl's middle. Tubbs now walked out of a darkened space and came over to them, resting his shoulders against the wall, his daughter resting an arm on his left shoulder. Tonight she was dressed very cultural: an Afrikan wrap with an embroidered long-sleeved T-shirt, and her head royally wrapped; the gold earrings she wore were matched in beauty by the almost illuminated Rasta embroidery she wore on her T-shirt. She was a very black sister and her skin glistened in the dim light, her eyes like starlets, or the irridescence of cats on a moonless night. This was about the fourth time Michael had seen them together, and each time he saw her she seemed to be a different person, a different personality. She looked regal and majestic, and Michael tried to look at her indifferently, but the jolt of her startling resemblance to the girl with the black scarf he had recently seen overwhelmed him.

"*The Messiah*", Tubbs said, "is well wicked. Irie irie. The man thumping some rassclaath music dey, I tell ya, it well fire me up! The man dread, I say, dread"!

"Put it dey mi idren"! Nose said, extending his open palm. "The bredder play some heavy cultural music, sah! Him deadly, me a-tell yo, deadly, iya. I man never did think say that I coulda get into dem different sounds dey, but it bring a lightness to I heart", thumping his chest, "me a tell yo. Tubbs, this bredder really wicked, wha ya say Rough Black"?!

"Yeah, the man wicked! Him really tough, is a experience, still".

"Seen", Tubbs nodded.

"The man dem want a guinness"? Nose asked, glancing at Stabber, he laughed again. Tubbs, his daughter, and Michael followed Nose's stare.

"The man enjoy himself, yo no see it, Rasta"?

"I man could well do with a guinness, Nose".

"How about the daughter"?

"Irie", she said, nodding her head.

Nose went off, pushing his way through the flock to get through. The music was deafening, but perceptively a scuffle could be heard outside. But this was a characteristic of the shebeen, and never precipitated any undue response among the flock. But a scream was heard, "Babylon, Babylon, Babylon, Babylon"! It sounded like the door was being kicked down, and immediately confusion and hysteria broke out. Everybody threw away their spliffs and members of the flock could be made out dipping in their pockets and throwing away folded newspaper. *The Messiah* was enraged! The flock broke up and people began to search for an exit. But as they surged forward, the police were already pushing and beating their way into the sweaty, humid rooms. Outside suddenly lit up as though the floodlights of a movie were now placed here, and they began to beam on the building. The police were snatching people in their pandemonium and fear. And *The Messiah* exploded!

"Which a we is the General? We can't let no bloodclaath Babylon mash down we fete. This is we ting. Stand firm, Black People! Stand firm! Don't throw down no bloodclaath arms, stand and defend your bloodclaath rights. This is war! Which a we is the General? Is the man dem General or pussyclaath cowards? Stand and defend your bloodclaath rights! Stand firm, Black People! London Bridge is fucking falling down and ley it go down in history that we sink it bloodclaath in the pussyclaath river. Ley we defend and show them bwoy who is the General? Is we a the General! Is we a the General! Is who a the General? A we a the General! . . ."

5

SHEBEEN AT DERELECT CROSSWAYS

The police were inside the building. There was no way to run except to the door or to the roof. The music was still playing. Stabber, Nose, *The Messiah*, Big Spliff (*The Messiah*'s right arm man) had all drawn their blades. As the police ran into the room, knocking people down and snatching them, the brethren started stabbing and cutting their way out. Police were falling and firing wildly with their batons which crashed against skulls, screams echoing like choked-up frights from horror films, but the police were also falling and screaming. Tubbs and Michael grabbed up two fallen batons and started to crash skulls. When Tubbs brought his baton down a policeman fell and was frothing through the mouth, simultaneously Michael crashed straight into a policeman's baton, shifted and the weight of it fell on his shoulder. He raised his hand up and across the policeman's face which sent him crashing to the ground and bleeding through the nose and head. The police were now trying to bring the dogs in. But *The Messiah* and Big Spliff had already drawn up contingency plans. They suddenly produced a bowl of dried red pepper and threw it at the dogs which started to sneeze and groan; now that they were helpless the brethren were attacking the police with a ferocity, hatred and anger that seemed to know no end. *The Messiah* and Big Spliff had two long five foot poles sharpened at the end and were now stabbing the dogs with them. The police fled outside. The fight had now moved to the street.

There must have been at least fifty policemen, about a quarter of whom were injured or incapacitated. Sirens and the noise of more police cars could be heard speeding up the derelict street. The music was still coming from inside. The streets were lit like day. Black people were beaten and thrown into vans. The brethren now looked like they were outnumbered, but a force of youths numbering well over a hundred were seen running up the street. The ferocity of their anger was preceded by bottles and stones which crashed into the windscreen of the police vans and cars, now wildly out of control and careering off the road. The police now feeling overwhelmed ran back into their vans, cars, motor bikes, taking off. Tubbs saw a policeman dragging his daughter on the ground as she struggled with him. He ran wildly into the policeman and crashed his baton onto his head and didn't stop until he was awashed with blood on the ground. He grabbed his daughter and moved back to the crowd. Police were now staggering. *The Messiah*, his head tied with a red handkerchief was ordering the flock to stone the Babylon and to destroy London Bridge. The vans, cars and motor bikes were leaping out of hell as bottles and stones crashed into the bright headlamps and floods that rested atop the vehicles.

As the police fled the scene, the flock started chanting A WE A THE GENERAL! A WE A THE GENERAL! A WE A THE GENERAL! Then the flock suddenly dispersed quietly and quickly as though obeying some secret inaudible order.

A tide and breath of cleanliness had now fallen over the derelict crossways . . . as though some heavenly blessing had been sent to restore dignity to a persecuted and brutalised people. A smell of blood and garbage assailed the air like some ancient ritual of battle and trial.

The early morning papers carried no news about the incident. Probably, Michael thought, because the incident happened at about 2 a.m. The radio was reporting the incident as early as four a.m., but the news was uninformed and brief. The reporter simply said that an incident of violence broke out between the police and black youths this morning when the police were attempting to enter premises that were alledged to be illegally used for the sale of drugs and unlicenced alcohol and suspected prostitution. Michael and Tubbs laughed when they had heard that. Michael's arm ached from the blow of the police baton and it was beginning to swell. He placed a towel into boiling water and rested it on his shoulder. He bawled as it burned and pained him. Tubbs' daughter was bruised, battered and scratched along her face and arm. She wanted to go to the hospital, but Tubbs said the police would be checking the hospitals for exactly that. He ran the bath and put her to lie down in the hot water. She was groaning from the pain of both the blows and the hot water. Tubbs massaged her body gently and she grimaced. After half an hour she came out and Tubbs made her lie on the bed and proceeded to massage her body with a mixture of Vicks vapour rub, soft candles, olive oil and black pepper. The mixture produced a burning sensation of her body, but she felt as though the pains were being sucked out by this magical concoction. She fell asleep exhausted and eroticised.

In the afternoon, both *The Evening Standard* and *The Evening News* ran stories with pictures of stabbed policemen, bandaged policemen, policemen being helped by their colleagues and a large picture of the Commissioner of police visiting the wounded and his statements to the press that justice will take its course and that the possibility of racial conflagration or deliberate confrontation with the police was to be dismissed. He also stated, and this was picked up by both newspapers, that the attack was executed by pimps and hustlers, people who were outcasts from the community and were indeed criminals (including drug pushers). Both accounts believed that historical relations between the police and black youths were responsible for the violence, and drew on incidents ranging from Liverpool to Notting Hill. One of the newspapers carried a page by an Asian journalist and community leader who stated that lack of government funds to community organizations should take the blame for the violence. He also detailed the high illiteracy rate amongst West Indians and the racism of schools to be partly responsible. Both Michael and Tubbs laughed at this, thinking this "coolie" was a cunt or a hustler.

In the evening the TV coverage was brief and almost indifferent. The following day the newspapers carried interviews with an array of Caribbean community leaders, self-appointed or otherwise, who uniformly attacked the racism of the police and of British society in general. None of the youths were interviewed or their own opinions reflected. There was no black journalist representing the black view. That same day the police invaded the Latimer Road area where the violence took place and were haughtily addressing any black youths they saw. They were in cars crawling lazily but meticulously around and on foot in twos. A number of innocent black youths were picked up under the SUS law. Many people understood this to be an attack on the black community in retaliation for what happened the night before. The police also got authorised search warrants to search the homes of a few of the well-known black youths who had previous records. There were isolated incidents of females and mothers being pushed about or slapped for refusing entry. The police also smashed a local shebeen and arrested a number of people for illegal possession and women for prostitution.

The arrested people, numbering about 13, were given bail and a defence committee was formed to raise money by holding rallies. It started off a few days after the incident by Jordan, Vidal, Ralph and some other brothers in Ladbroke Grove. The reports in the press did not die away, but were kept up at a steady pace. The tone of the articles was that of sympathy, the line being that Caribbean youth were alienated from British society by its racism and its culture that threatened their identity. The defence committee issued a statement to the press that was only marginally reflected in the various press reports, being kept to a short quote or a paragraph. This was anticipated, but the committee members thought it prudent that they should go on record as responding both to the incident and the slant of the press reports. Ralph suggested that a copy should be sent to the Home Office and to the Commissioner of Police. They were sent and brief notes of acknowledgement were remitted within a week.

Michael hung on to his job, but had already made his mind up that he was leaving. A vague flicker of light was touching the back of his head: he felt sufficiently experienced to go back to school and do some studying. With all the decisions that he had come to, his professional inadequacy was at the back of his mind. He reasoned that he could not continue to be violent without some kind of construction in his own life. That if violence was coupled with some kind of activity, he would feel better. The idea had occurred to him in his sporadic forays into the community centre's library where he would constantly hear heated discussion and saw that not all grown-ups were old farts like his father. These men demonstrated real concern for the lives of the young and he felt motivated by what he had heard and learnt. The more he read was the more liberated he became. The little facts about the meaning of dreadlocks in Afrika and its origins in Jamaica expanded his understanding and made him feel more responsible. In fact one of the brethren who worked in the Centre was beginning to show some interest in him. Thus he was opening up himself to influence and guidance. He also started attending lectures by black speakers, but the information they gave was muddled because of the language and the posh accents that they employed. He felt frustrated by this, but not defeated.

Like a lot of youths, Michael was preoccupied with his physique and ability to be fit. This had led him, Tubbs, Stabber, Nose and some others to attend late night Kung Fu movies. Each time a new one came out, they would all pile into somebody's car and take off. The next day, after work, they would sometimes get together in somebody's flat or at the local community centre in Harlesden where they attempted to imitate Bruce Lee's devastatingly deadly moves. A Kung Fu class had also started up, supervised by a white man, but very few people had turned up, and after six weeks it folded. The warden then casually asked Nose the reason for its failure and discovered that the brethren would not accept a white man. Within three weeks, a black man, a continental Afrikan (from Ghana), was found. The man was gentle, strict, forceful and skillful. Over twenty youths immediately joined up.

They all sweated, poked, kicked, screamed, threw each other, capsised, laughed and received injuries, but it made them feel proud of their physical strength, skill and their bodies, becoming even more contoured, muscled, healthy and vigorous. Michael would go back to his room, take off his clothes and made all kinds of poses before the mirror. He felt good, but his face looked still too young, he felt. He would be sixteen in two months, and he felt his baby face betrayed his ambitions.

Nose started to show an interest in music and got a bass guitar from one of his contacts for £40. It was a red fender and Nose started walking all over the place with it. He started rehearsing at home and was being given some lessons by Winston Jones, the bassist with *The Staff of JAH*, a Reggae band that achieved a great deal of Roots appeal in two years. Nose was anxious to learn and picked up the rudiments very quickly. Everybody thought it was strange how Nose had switched so suddenly and quickly, but Michael, Tubbs and Stabber realised that Nose recognized that women were more accessible if he played in a band. Some of the prettiest daughters would hook up with a brother because he played in a band. It had nothing to do with the quality of the brother's looks, attitudes or ability, but the connection with the band, as though the glamour rubbed off on the daughters themselves, and that their own insulated and unimportant condition took on a certain power and radiance and meaning.

The brethren would go round to Nose's place on some afternoons and watch him practise. Almost invariably other professional or budding musicians turned up and would plug in a guitar and start to jam. There was always drums in Nose's flat (one huge room in which he was squatting) and anybody would start to drum Rasta rhythms on them. Michael was looking on for a long time before attempting to play. He observed microscopically and assimilated the different beats, rhythm, timing and tempos. Then he started drumming once or twice a week. Daughters started turning up once they heard a jam was constantly happening at Nose's place. They would come and sit, some to wait for their man, but mostly to be part of the feeling of connection, identity and a bond with a musician.

It was a cold spring afternoon, the wind blowing like dragons, the air with that smell of budding life and the skies turning a pale blue from a nasty white/grey . . . Michael went down in Nose's flat to jam or to listen, and saw the daughter immediately as he entered. She was wearing a white shawl/scarf exactly the same way when he first saw her, around her head and draped over her shoulders; white Indian blouse, a long black skirt beneath which was thick black tights fitted into a pair of brown kicker boots. Michael nearly jumped out of his skin and immediately felt jealous, nervous and violent. Winston Jones was playing bass, another brother on guitar and three other youths were in the room, including Nose. Michael moved as far away from her as possible and stood with his head bowed taking in the scene. No words were being exchanged and the vibrations were a little heavy, a little tense. Michael was so overwhelmed by the daughter's presence that he did not even notice that it was Tubbs' daughter, Levi (her name was Miranda, but she preferred to be called by her Twelve Tribes name, the month in which she was born) who was sitting next to her. Winston seemed to be in deep concentration, a spliff, unlit, hanging on his lips, going into a state of meditation, as the sounds/melo-ridims he produced described some lighted tropical field far away . . .

An inner voice entered Michael's mind and he felt compellingly drawn to the drums, his mind already walking across the room, as though a force had taken control of his spirit and was magnetising him to a spiritual expression, to unearth the turbulent feelings that played and preyed in his skull. Then rationalism took over, suppressing it, bringing a feeling of inferiority, inability to match the zenith of ability shown here . . . "Rough Black", Michael heard his name called and saw Winston Jones pointing to him with his index finger and then to the drums. He did this twice and he walked over forgetting his fear or confusion. The music was sailing on a feeling coloured by reflection and idealism. He came in hesitatingly, but on time, feeling the tempo, trying to integrate himself into the vibe/feel and the spirit. As his palm hit the skins he felt a hot emotion swelling in his head, the music going into distant lands; find the colour, the colour, the colour, he told himself. Feel the smell of the land, the land. Yes, yes, yes, reflect it, express it, yes, yes . . .

Winston was now smiling, satisfied and jubilant, the Rasta ridim now flooding his soul, overpowering him, and his own melodic chants came over with a deeper, softer groundedness, earthiness, flowed melifluously, and with the articulate power of authority and command. Michael drummed, his hands as though controlled by some other person or thing manifesting a steady and improvised rhythm. His head was bowed over the drum/repeater and he found that by closing his eyes the rhythm came up with greater clarity, with just darkness and feeling in his mind. Without knowing it the two daughters were clapping in time and soon began to hum in a deep guttural religious way that brought forth memories of his mother's singing. The music now seemed to characterize a power of its own, that was balanced, symmetrical and polyrhythmic, driving the soul into a kind of ecstatic state of beingness, transporting it to some place where memory and mind-matter was free . . . to ruminate, to recall, to visualise and envision. It was a kind of freedom he had never experienced and he did not want it to end. He saw the whole of history, the whole of Afrika, the whole of the Caribbean and Black America, the wholeness and oneness of the total black experience, a whole tradition of life unfolding in his brain as a river flows uninterruptedly into the sea, flowing, flowing . . . "JAH"! he heard something in his voice said, as the sweat poured off his taut, emotionally torn face. And the room alighted with "RASTAFARI"! His eyes were closed, but he suddenly opened them and saw that the others were turned into themselves, taken away on this wave of beauty and feeling. It was another five minutes before the music came to an end, the bass doing a melodic passage and falling out, the guitar gave a sharp final shout and stopped, and Michael hit the skins in a prayer-like tribute and also ended. Winston was already slapping palms with the other brother on guitar and came over with a broad smile, extending his palm for Michael to slap it. "Rough Black"! he said, returning Michael's slap and then closing his palm over Michael's and shaking them tightly. The daughters were nodding their heads, eyes opened and saying "Rastafari" very quietly as though talking to themselves. They were now nodding in Michael's direction. Michael nodded back, but felt a little embarrassed. Levi/Miranda waved him over and introduced him to her friend.

"This daughter is a Asher, and her name is Cherri".

"Hail", Michael said, nodding his head.

"Love brethren", Cherri said, her face unsmiling, but friendly and peaceful. "The man will like a draw"?

"Love", Michael said, nodding again.

Winston was talking to the guitarist and waved Michael over. The guitarist was a stockily built brother and had a powerful physique.

"This man is Moses", Winston said to Michael. They shook hands and nodded to each other.

"This man is Rough Black", Winston said to Moses. "The man come a long way. You really played beautiful, man. You ready now to join a band. That is the next step".

"Praises to the I", Moses said, "the man is truly ready".

Michael laughed and it slowly turned into a grin, his heart feeling jubilant and self-satisfied, but he knew he could never really be part of a band.

"I man well appreciate the praises", he said, laughing again, "but I man not really a professional musician. Is just the spirit that take I, you know. Is just a vibe, a feeling. I man don't know if I could repeat it".

"Still", Winston said, "its something to cultivate. Once the man reach dem spiritual heights, the Father is watching and guiding the man. So if the man buckle down to some hard work, you never know what can happen".

"Seen", Moses said.

"Seen", Michael said.

The daughters were smoking the spliff and Winston lit his own. Cherri brought the spliff over to Michael, then walked back to Levi.

"Ises", Michael said, and inhaled. He had a smile on his face. He was wondering how he could handle the situation of Cherri, communicating to her without being overbearing or obvious. It was obvious, he knew, that she liked him. The difference in their ages kept coming to him like a meteor. But she certainly didn't act like there was any difference between them, and both Winston and Moses who were over twenty treated him like an equal, somewhat small-brotherish, but with obvious respect and affection. Sometimes people told him he looked 18 which made him feel good. In appearance Cherri looked like 17, but her attention to dress and behaviour demonstrated to Michael that she had to be older.

Moses, after passing the draw back to Winston, said he had to shift. Winston, now looking at his watch, said that he too should be attending rehearsals. They both left together, and Nose entered the room, saying "Love, man. Sight the man dem soon", to Winston and Moses. Michael felt a slight stab in his chest because he felt that Nose must be after Cherri. He was standing in the same place and decided to walk over and hail Levi. Nose touched both Levi and Cherri on the arm and asked them if they were alright. They uniformly said yes. He hailed Michael and was chatting to him when the doorbell rang. He left to answer it. Michael then seized the opportunity to walk over to the daughters and converse.

"This a nice draw", he said to them both.

"Yeah, I got it from Tubbs. He musta got it from the Youth, you know the youth with the funny eyes".

"Yeah. He does have some nice smoke".

"The man knock the repeater well hard", Cherri said with admiration.

"Well, is just the inspiration from Winston and Moses, you know. They gave me the spirit and I just go deh. But I am not really a drummer, but still try, you know".

"Still, that is really something", she said, smiling.

"Yes, Michael", Levi said, "You should really take it up a little more seriously. Even Tubbs who's been playing longer than you, is not that good, really".

Michael laughed and shook his head, thinking how to reply.

"Tubbs is a carpenter, a craftsman, not a musician, really. And he never take anything serious but him work, you know. And I now, is just pure accident that I man felt that vibe. Just inspiration, really. But I man doubt that I could repeat it".

"Give praises still", Cherri said, her face serious, "the Father holds the key".

"Seen", they both agreed. There was something about Cherri that frightened Michael. She was deadly serious where most people were half-joking most of the time. Even he did not feel completely convinced, but went along because it propelled the crisis within him to some kind of solution, some kind of resolution. A few of his Rasta friends were really serious and dedicated, but most were unsure, uncertain, and indecisive about the absoluteness of their commitment.

At that moment Nose entered with a friend and they went straight to the instruments, setting up a vibe, a feeling. Michael felt himself relax and sat there with Cherri and Levi feeling the world taking on some meaning, some life, some radiance that was touching him, turning him . . . And he recognized that the warmth of that feeling was the communicated feeling between him and Cherri, that unspoken something that he felt, like they both shared something indescribable, but pure and idealistic that they longed and searched for. As the smoke entered his lungs and brain he felt light and powerful, and his spirit felt clean and his mind a soft waterfall, running smoothly down the mountainside, emptying its beautiful tears unto the world . . .

6

FAMILY REUNION

Josie had sent him a brithday present through his sister Roberta. There was also a card, the inside printed with a short verse, corny, but sweet and thoughtful. When he opened the gift-wrapped package, there was a set of three underpants, three pairs of socks, a T-shirt and a pair of trousers. It touched him. Roberta kept looking at the room, with surprise and wonder.

"Tell my mother thanks. It's really nice. I like it, but she shouldn't a bothered. I'm alright".

"I could see that. Boy your room look nice, yes. You must be doing alright".

"Well, I'm working, you know".

"Yuh sure you working and not with them friends of yours"?

"Course I'm working. You wanta see my payslip"?

"Well, you sure looking alright".

"I make £35 a week. Not bad. My rent is £10, and most times I eat by Tubbs' mum. She cook some good food".

"You looking really good. God, and you growing so tall, boy! Just now you go look like a lamp post"!

"Well, you can't expect me to stay a baby all mi life".

"You getting that mannish look in yuh face like yuh well doing yuh tings"!

"God, you're so nosey. You ain change at all".

"Well, you is muh brother, I must ask you. You have a nice girl nah"?

"Who tell you I have girl nah"! He affected a Dominican accent and they both laughed.

"But look at my crosses. This boy become one big man, eh"!

"So how you and William doing"?

"That's what I come to tell you about. We getting engaged on the 5th of next month. So mama ask me to tell you . . . and I wanted to invite you too. We having a little reception in the house, a little family ting and we thought you should be there, Rasta an all". When she made the last remark a twinkle came into her eye, communicating to Michael that it was a tease.

"And what about dad"?

"What about him"?

"How he feel about all this? He won't object to my locks"?

"Which locks"? She knocked his tam off. "That little picky head you calling locks. That ting ain start to grow yet, boy".

He slapped her hand and she hit him back. He slapped her hand again and she threw him on the bed on which they were sitting. Then she jumped on him and held his arms. He put his foot between her thighs and tried to toss her over, but she pressed her weight against him. He moved from side to side, but he couldn't get her off. Then he put one foot around her thighs, sliding them onto her bottom and started wiggling them. She started laughing and weakening her grip. He easily pushed her off, snatched up a pillow and banged her head with it. She laughed so much that she was crying. He hit her for a few more minutes and stopped.

"That show you not to play with a big man"! He stood on the floor guffing out his chest and hitting it with both hands. She sat up, wiping her tears, then with a sudden motion, she picked up the pillow and flung it at him, but just as quickly he ducked and it crashed into the wall.

"Too fast for you, girl".

"Michael, you're a damn devil. Yuh only got me because you know I ticklish. You ain stronger than me nah. I stronger. You're a cheat. You always used to do that. That's the only way you could win a fight, by tickling people. You know something? I miss that, you know, all that romping we used to do together. Sam and Evelyn and them too young for me to play with".

"But what you need people to play with when you have William. Eh"?

"Shut yuh damn mout! William is not muh brother".

"So what"?

"Mind your own business"!

"So I guess everybody is happy now? You getting engaged and that, ole Josie must be feeling well proud".

"Well you have to get engaged and married at some time. You might as well start now. But I can't get over it, you know, you looking really good. You must have some young girl looking after you, eh"?

"Nah. I do everything myself. Is just I man, yo no see it, daughtah"!

"Yo no see it, daughtah! All you could talk stupid, yes"!

"William ain no fool, you know. He knows everything that is happening. So don't pretend he don't talk like that to you, even in a joke".

"He does try, but is not him really. That don't suit him at all nah".

"So how everybody at home then"?

"Everybody is well, yes, but that Eve is going to be one trouble maker. You know how she fast aready. When William come, she all up in de man face. If I don't tell her to go inside, she won't leave, you know".

"She take after you"?

"Take after me! I was never like that chile, never"!

"So mum still short tempered? Still troubling the children"?

"Mama is not that bad, you know. All you have to do is understand her. And she easy to understand. When a person is a certain way and they not going to change, you have to try and understand them. She was brought up in a certain way and she just can't help the way she is".

"Oh yeah. She will get a bad heart if she don't stop upsetting herself. Easy to get a heart attack, you know. She don't understand her children . . ."

"You really can't say that, Michael. You know, this world we live in have a lot of pressures and people release it in different ways. You know, that's mama way of releasing it, shouting and bawling, but she's just as concerned. It's just that's the way she carry on. You can't hold that against her all your life. You have to forgive and forget".

"I just don't like the way they treated me, that's all. All this fuss about my locks and bloodclaath school"!

"Michael"!

"Yeh. Is people like dem that make their kids turn out bad. If you can't relate to your kids, you shouldn't have none. Don't complain if you have four or five kids and take your pressures out on them and then say is the pressures. You should know what you want and stick to it".

"Yes, yes, I agree with you, but . . ."

"I didn't want go to school. All that shit I was taking from them racist bloodclaath teachers! I shoulda beat dem up, that's what I shoulda done".

"You sound so bitter, Michael. You must have been thinking this all along".

"Course I was! What d'you expect? You expect me to be kind hearted and understanding when nobody is kind and understanding to me? It's the worst ting to have your parents not being on your side. You feel deserted like. There's nobody to turn to except your friends. And my friends are now my family. They show more concern for me than my family. With mum and dad it's do what I say or get out. What d'you expect? Still, I'll come to the engagement. At least I'll give it some thought. But if I come, I'll bring a couple of my friends. And I know what they will say: get the Rastas out"!

"Oh don't be like that, Michael. It's my engagement. I have a say in who comes and who don't. If you want to bring a couple of friends, there's no harm in that. You mustn't get so bitter. You'll drown in your own tears".

"Well, you'll be surprised. A lot of people will be surprised, you'll see. I have a few ideas, but I ain saying nothin just yet. I'm just waiting for time. Tell them I'm alright. Not to worry. Ain't I taking care of myself"?

"You certainly are. I'm surprised, no, I shouldn't be because you was never really untidy, just a bit lazy, that's all. But your place is clean and looking good. Tell me nah, you have a girl friend"?

"Nosey, nosey", he said tapping his nose and smiling. "You talk about Eve, but you're just as bad. Keep your nose out of my business".

"Awright, be like that then". She was now feigning to be hurt.

But Michael knew that even though she was pretending she really wanted to discover his secrets. But he was not prepared to tell her. "So what you gon buy me for my engagement then"?

"Well, I think I'll get you a Rasta tam"!

"You must be joking, mate"! She laughed scandalously and slapped his arm.

"You shouldn't ask me then. Don't worry, I'll get you something. Some eggs, maybe, you can put them to hatch, and if you wait long enough, you'll probably get some babies"!

"Oh Michael, stop your damn teasing. I'm not having any baby. Feel my belly. It's flat".

"Oh forget it. It's only a tease. Can't you take a joke? You like to give, but you can't take, eh"?

"Oh I better be going, Michael. I got some sewing to do at home. You want me to do anything for you before I go"?

"Nothin I can think of really. I don't know . . ."

"Well, do you need any trousers to darn? Or shirts, anything. You want me to wash anything for you"?

"Nah, I'm awright, Roberta. Everything is under control. Dread at the control, you no see it"?

"Well, alright then. I'm going. Imagine, I haven't seen you in six months. Boy, you're really wayward and own way"!

After the meeting with Cherri at Nose's flat, Michael ran into her on more than one occasion, each time they would make small talk, but Cherri had an intense way of talking and looking, as though her very existence depended on her words. Michael, of course, was puzzled by her emotions, but could not work out a reason for it. She was a very nice beautiful attractive woman and when he was with her it made him feel comfortable and good. Then one day he was coming from work on the tube and saw her at Piccadilly Circus changing to the Bakerloo line. He followed until she stopped to wait for the train on the platform. Then he walked up to her surreptiously and stood by her side. She quickly turned around.

"Oh"! she looked surprised, "I felt the presence, but too late. Maybe I was too deep in thought". Then her hand reached out and touched his shoulder gently resting there for a second or two. His sister Roberta had the very same habit. On rush hour the platform was crowded, you had to inch your way along or push your way through.

"Sorry. I just meant to surprise the daughtah".

"Well, you did. And how are you"? She removed her hand from his shoulder and placed it on her chest. Michael looked at her delicate thin fingers. Her wrist, thin and bony, tapered beautifully into her hands. She wore no make-up except for something that looked like mascara, but it was an Indian material that a few of the daughters used which was said to protect the eyes from dust. There was also another type that came in a stick that Indians (Asians) also used to clean their eyes. On her it was very black and contrasted with her complexion, a light brown but full of hue and colour. The jumper she wore looked Mexican. A lot of white people wore them, very few blacks. It was very thick and had a hood dangling at the back of her thin neck. She wore a beaded necklace in Rasta colours, but they were fine and delicate and her wrist held about eight bracelets on one hand, the other an Afrikan leather bracelet.

"I man cool".

"That's all. Cool"? They both laughed. Her eyes opened out. "What were you doing in these parts"?

"O, I work more or less in the area, you know". He felt embarrassed because he thought her next question would be what work he did. But she didn't ask that. Her mind wavered for a minute, then connected.

"What do you do with yourself most of the time, I mean after work"?

"Mess around" . . .

"What does mess around mean, eh"?

"Well, I do a few things"?

"Like what"? Michael felt a little cowed. She was very aggressive.

"Well, for one, like most youth I'm into karate, right. I do a bit of reading, visiting friends, go to the pictures sometimes, check Nose out and mess wth the drums, or see Tubbs, talk and have a smoke. What's that to you anyway"? He felt his own aggression now rising in him.

"I'm only curious. When you say read, what type of books you read? Maybe you can recommend some to me".

"Well, I'm only just starting myself. But I read a bit about black history and culture. That sort of thing".

"Hhhhhhmmmmmmmm". She looked thoughtful and reflective, her eyes momentarily closing. "Yes. That is interesting". When she said that a smile broke her face. This was the first time Michael had ever seen this side of her personality and it frightened him a little bit. He always thought that there was something strange about her, but he never knew it was this. She was actually questioning him like a supervisor or something. Before they could continue the conversation, the train came in. They pushed their way into a *No Smoking* carriage and stood up holding onto a leather support. Each time the train took a bend, she rocked against him, or when it came to a sudden halt, she rolled back onto him. Her body felt soft tender and beautiful. It sparked emotion in his head. The train came to Baker Street and they changed for the Metropolitan Line. They walked silently, with people rushing up the escalator and pushing past them. Even though he did this every day, he hated it. It took more than five minutes to walk over to the Metropolitan Line. He was feeling hot and sweaty. Summer was near. It could be felt in the air and its smell of leaves, but here on the underground there was sweat dirt and pacing bodies.

He wondered why he had come this way, but if asked he could always make up an excuse, saying that he was going to see a friend. But when they reached the platform, the Hammersmith train pulled in, and as they sat down she turned her head to the window, looking out.

"Would you like a draw"? She said it so casually, he pretended he didn't hear.

"What did you say"? She still looked through the window.

"Would you like a draw"?

"Yeh. That would be nice".

"I have some at home. If you're not doing anything, you can stop by and have a smoke with me".

"As a matter of fact I have some on me now".

"Yeah"?

"I forgot it on me from last night. This is the same pair of trousers I had on from yesterday".

"I live in Shepherd's Bush with my father".

"With your father"? Her head slowly turned away from the window.

"Yes, with my father. My mother and father separated since I was five years old. My mother used to live in this country, but after they separated, she lived here for a number of years until I was eleven, then she left for home and has never returned".

"Your mother is smart".

"How do you mean then"?

"Well, Rasta want return home. She ups and digs out. That's good".

"It's good, but it hasn't been that good for me".

"I don't live with my parents. I left home nine months ago. I don't ever see either of them except if my mother comes to see me. And that's not often. To tell you the truth I don't miss them at all. It was my decision to leave home. And I'm glad I did. It made me more responsible like. I had to see about myself for a change. That's good. My friends stood by me and I'm awright. I ain got nothin to worry about except myself".

"You sound like you're boasting. But I guess it's a prideful thing, to make it on your own. Then again you had parents to leave. I didn't have both".

"What difference does it make? Ain't no difference. Whether they there or not there, it's the caring that counts. Does your dad care about you"?

"Yes, he does very much. We get along fine".

They got off at Shepherd's Bush. She was going to wait for a bus, but Michael said that they should walk. She opened up to him and he in turn told a lot about his life. It was a block of recently built Council flats, way off the Uxbridge Road. The surroundings were unusually clean for Council flats, even the lift was piss and smell free. In fact it was clean. Michael wondered what type of people lived here. It was obvious to him it wasn't privately owned. They reached the top floor, six, walked through a swinging door, turned right again and walked through another swinging door to 61F. She opened it and he was surprised to find the place comfortably and tastefully furnished. The corridor had thick pile carpet with reproductions framed on the walls. She took her shoes off in front of her room, and Michael felt that he had too as well, but she told him he didn't have to. When he entered the room, he took his shoes off and placed them against the wall. Her room was also lushly carpeted two mattresses resting on the floor covered with a quilt, at the end of the bed there was a piece of Afrikan cloth folded. There was about four huge cushions in different parts of the room, a small stool that looked South American. On the walls were poem-posters, one with the Afrikan's Prayer, and oil paintings. The thing that fascinated him the most was a small framed picture of an Ethiopian in what looked like a strange pose. He saw pictures like that in the books he read. There was also a big piece of Afrikan sculpture in one corner and an embroided bird on the wall above it.

He felt cowed by the opulence of the room and of the easiness with which Cherri moved in it. She sat on the edge of the bed and folded her legs like a Buddha, her long dress rising up over her legs which she pulled down over her bent knees. He sat on a cushion and took out some smoke, the remnants of a £10 draw. Before he could ask for papers, she pointed to a painted ceramic bowl, he reached for it and saw big and small papers, but not the ordinary rizla, but those that they sold in the hippie shops and were expensive, a small pipe, folded newspaper in a cellophane bag (it must be smoke, he thought) and other stuff. She got up and put a cassette on. It was a Sansui cassette deck, finished in black, and two wharfdale speakers brought the sound of Burning Spear to him. She went back to the bed, sitting in the same position. He passed some smoke to her, but she asked him for the pipe. She placed some ganja in the small pipe, packing it tight, lit it and inhaled. He meticulously rolled his joint, making a long thin one, lit it and inhaled.

The music spoke with a deep spirituality and concern. They smoked silently, Michael's nervousness wearing away with each inhalation. Cherri threw her head back each time she sucked from the pipe and inhaled. The symbolic language of the music was more powerful than any words could communicate. The rhythm took on ancient dimensions, the Spear testifying like he was in some traditional church of the spirit, or testifying through the spirit itself. The words were not long and complicated like Bob Marley's but each one created a vast mural of intricately woven designs, assembling in the mind the vastness and dimension of *time, place and the moment*. Everything could be seen, felt and reacted to: history was before his eyes/her eyes; the past unfolded like a film, brought before the present to look at, examine, touch and feel.

Feeling, ah, that was the *word*, the ability to connect with one's own spirit, one's own reality and self, that brought other feelings and emotions or pictures into living reality. The Spear's music was as real to them as the room they sat in. Each inhalation of ganja brought the spirit of time and history closer into grasp and understanding. The room's warmth, its fineness, its decorations and *colour* aided in the persuasion of the emotions . . . lighting up most microscopic of feeling feeling.

When her pipe went out, she tried relighting, but the ganja had burnt itself out. He passed the ashtray to her, she knocked the pipe with her index finger and the ash fell into the tray, then she took the used match and cleaned it out. He passed his smoke to her and she took it between her thin bony fingers and put it to her mouth. Michael closed his eyes and rested against the cushion, stretching his feet out. He must have dozed off, for when he opened his eyes, she was lying on the bed and Ras Michael & the Sons of Negus was playing on the cassette. Her hands were behind her head, her long sleeved T-shirt was not on and a sleeveless T-shirt (which must have been underneath) showed her delicately pointed breasts. They looked small, but perfectly rounded and pointed to the tip of her nipples; the long dress she wore arched where her pubic area was, her legs bent at the knees and one resting on the other a little above the ankles. Michael looked at her neck, her breasts, her waist, the little arch that protruded from her middle and the small shiny moulded calves and ankles. He rose up and rolled another spliff. When she heard him move, her eyes flew open and she shifted her head to face him.

"You fell asleep, you know that? Are you hungry"?

"I musta been more tired than I knew. I stayed up until three this morning, smoking and playing dominoes. Then I got up at eight to get ready for work".

"You play dominoes well"?

"Not bad. My father is good at it though".

"But are you hungry"?

"Well, I I I. . . . are you gonna eat? . . . what time is it . . . if you are, I will".

"It's ten to seven . . ."

"What?! So late! . . ."

"You have something to do"?

"No, I just didn't realise it was so late, that's all. Where's your father"?

"Oh he has a woman and after work he sometimes stays there or he phones to say if he's not coming home".

"What does your dad do for a living"?

"He's a civil servant really, but he dabbles in art . . . collects things, talks about things with his friends and he writes a little bit. I guess he must have given it up, but it's his interest now, you know. Are you hungry"?

"Well, I'll eat if you're eating. Man cool, you know, but if the daughtah don't want to eat, it still cool".

"Well, I'm not very hungry, but I feel to eat something. What do you want to eat"?

"Anything really. I'm not fussy".

"OK, I'll fix us something small".

When she left the room, Michael got up and looked around. There was knitting needles on a small wooden shelf behind the mattresses, books (when he flicked through them, they were mainly about women, anatomy, rearing children, etc.), an unfinished knitted tank top and an embroidery pattern onto cloth that looked like it was just started. He felt as though Cherri was into this woman lib thing that the brethren dismissed as being lesbianism, but she certainly acted quite normally, or perhaps better than normal. He picked up the book on anatomy, started to flick through it, sat on the cushion, read bits and pieces, put it down, rolled a joint, smoked, searched for a cassette, placed it in the deck, smoked , sat on the cushion and smoked, then a slow gripping darkness entered his head, sucking him into sleep which he fought, it held him, he relit the spliff, smoked, darkness gripped him like an angel of death, he woke up, put the spliff down, and fell back to sleep.

When Cherri returned to the room forty minutes later she saw him sleeping, placed the places on mats on thefloor, returned to the kitchen with juice on coasters, placed them on the floor, then shook him gently. He opened his eyes and closed them again. She shook him again, saying his name. His eyes flew open, and he sat up.

"The food is ready, Michael".

"Let me use your toilet", he said, rubbing his eyes. She showed him where it was. The toilet and bathroom were together, but the softness of the room told him that they must have decorated it with their own money. The room was painted blue, there was a shower over the bath, blue plastic curtains, blue tiles on the other side of the bath tub, and wooden pine towel racks behind the door and shelves on the wall, with a pine medicine cabinet and two spot-lights. When he had washed his face and rinsed his mouth, he returned to the room to find that Cherri hadn't touched her food. He sat on the cushion and it was only when he started to eat that she touched the food.

There were boiled potatoes with butter, boiled cabbage and carrots with butter, lentils and brown rice, with a salad that had apple and avocado. He ate with a relish and appeasement, the food entering his stomach with a smoothness. It was a soft meal and he felt a deep admiration for this woman. When he had finished, she was still eating and asked him if he wanted more, he refused, but she asked again and he accepted. She took his plate and returned, placing it in his hand. He ate ravishingly, his embarrassment wearing away. They finished almost simultaneously. Then he drank his juice, placed the glass down and rolled another joint.

"You wanta try the pipe"? He nodded and she passed it to him. He lit it, smoked and passed it to her. She inhaled twice and passed it back. She now finished the juice. When he had finished the juice, she took everything up and took them to the kitchen. He refilled the pipe and smoked again. She must be washing up, he thought. He went over to the bed, sat, then stretched out. He smoked and dreamed dreams. Ahh, this life, this world . . . Ahh, this daughtah is real nice, a real nice girl, mmmmmmm . . . He was sleeping again. He fought it, sleep gripped him, fought it, sleep gripped him . . .

When he woke up, he had lost his sense of geography and place. He didn't know where he was. His eyes opened and as though some voice was talking to him, some weird, instantly forgettable dream was activating his consciousness to awake, and his senses reeled, confused, turned, and it came to him in the blackness that engulfed the room. When he tried to get up, he realised he was under the bedcovers fully clothed, and an arm was resting on his chest and a head next to him. He realised now that it was Cherri's, for a moment he thought it was Roberta he was sleeping with. She sometimes had the habit of coming into bed with him when she herself couldn't sleep. When he was up to twelve, he didn't mind it, but as he grew older he told her so. She did it less, but still came to his bed sporadically. The way Cherri held him it made him feel like her brother. He wondered what time it was, where her father was, and what would he say when he found him in her room. This made him feel uneasy, both for his safety and for Cherri's. He held her hand gently, placed it at her side, and got out of the bed. What he got out of the bed for, he didn't know. But he got up and fumbled around until he hit something on the floor, a glass perhaps, and Cherri turned and was awakened. She called his name and he whispered to her. She asked him if he wanted something, and he said no. She asked if he wanted the light on and he said yes. She searched behind the mattress and switched a red light on from the mains. She told him to come over and sit down. He obeyed her. He sat down.

"I saw you were tired and asleep, so I put you under the sheets".

"You shoulda wake me up".

"Well, I didn't want to. You looked so tired".

"Is your father home"?

"I don't know. When I came to bed at ten, he hadn't turned up, nor did he ring. If he is, he would probably be sleeping".

"What if he finds out I'm here"?

"Oh, he won't find out. I have my privacy. Why don't you come to bed, you got to work tomorrow, haven't you"?

"Yeah, OK". He sat on the bed, hesitating. She told him he could take his clothes off and be more comfortable, that she had a pair of pyjamas that might fit him. After a long burdensome silence, he consented. She was about to get out of bed, and he asked her to show him where. She pointed to a corner of the room, on top a small trunk. He found them, changed his clothes and got into bed, keeping his underpants on. He didn't know what time it was and that bothered him. He laid down in the soft and comfortable bed feeling slightly confused about Cherri. He didn't know whether she was after sexual intercourse or she was just simple. After about five minutes of thought she rested her arm on his chest, snuggled her head between his shoulder and head, and fell asleep. Michael was thinking and felt trapped in the bed, as though her hands were weighing a ton. He felt like lifting her arm, actually followed the thought to touching it, then changed his mind. Then he thought about Bunting, a girl he hadn't seen in two years and wondered what had become of her. It was this thought that sent him finally to sleep. The room had felt like a warm belly into which he had now climbed and its softness, warmth and tender spirit had taken his childhood into a deep restful dark softness where dreams and reality merged together as indivorceable twins.

At first Michael thought of Cherri as a close friend, but as they came closer, he saw her as his woman. They had been seeing each other constantly for about a month, returned from a party late at night, and his place was far away from Ealing. The nearest stop would be Cherri's, but the thought of her father disturbed him. He didn't want to be seen as disrespectful. He was stoned out of his mind and felt like he was walking two inches above the ground. She put her arm around his waist and walked to the mini cab office. There were two guys, an old and a young one. The old guy was grumpy, mean and nasty and said they won't have a car for an hour, but the young one said that Jimmy had just come in, but was having a tea. The old guy said that Jimmy had to pick up a customer, the young guy said that he had already sent Tom for that. Both Cherri and Michael were showing silent anger at the old man. The young one then pointed out the green escort and they went over to it. They drove in silence, Michaell resting against the seat feeling life was a golden cloud, a shower of yellow light . . .

Cherri had paid the man an astonishing £3.75. She felt cheated and shoved £4 in the man's hands. She didn't want to argue. The man was black. She walked with her arm around Michael's waist to the lift, up to the sixth floor, and told him to wait until she checked whether her father was at home. As she flicked on the light she saw a note on the floor, "Won't be back until tomorrow, Daddy". She beckoned Michael in and they went straight to her room. She went to the bathroom, spent about ten minutes and came back. She removed Michael's shoes, then changed into a white long nightdress. She had taken all her clothes off except her panties. She asked Michael if he wanted to wear her pyjamas again, and he said he would, but would rest for a while. She went under the covers, with Michael resting on top. A few minutes passed, then she put her arm around his chest, this time she didn't leave her hands dead, they were gently rubbing his chest, searching for his nipples, rubbing them gently with her finger-tips, and they responded with a firmness that he never knew he possessed. She leaned over and rested her head on his chest, then unbuttoned his shirt, still gently massaging his nipples, a hot burning sensation covering his face, his neck, his thighs quivering, and his penis breaking up in his trousers. He turned around and suddenly pulled her by the hair, raising her up and then down on his mouth, kissing her lips, warm soft and responsive. She placed her tongue in his mouth and moved them feebly about. He returned it with violent thrusts. Her fingers still massaged his nipples, then her entire palm went over them. Michael pushed her off him and laid on top of her chest, she gasped for breath and he became a little gentler, slipping his hands into her bosom, feeling those already firm hardened cashew nuts, warming and burning his fingers, passing them now over her entire breasts, feeling the smallness, shape and softness of them. She moved her hand into his trousers, but they couldn't go far enough. He unbuckled his belt and unzipped his trousers, her fingers searching for his penis. When she felt it, firm and like the muscle of an arm, she gave a small inaudible sigh. Michael let go of her mouth, emotion possessing him, beating him, strangling him, taking away his breath, and he allowed his passion to follow the trace of her neck, chest and onto her breasts. He seized them between his lips and kissed kissed them, licked them, kissed and licked them. She massaged his penis gently, then pulled hard on his foreskin and it began to burn and hurt him, but he liked and wanted it. A juice came up out of the head of his penis, but he didn't know although Cherri felt her fingers wet and she rubbed the juice over his stiff head, rubbed it, massaged it, squeezed it, rubbed it, then began to pull his trousers down. She rose up and pulled them down. He took off the rest and went under the covers. She went under with him and he undressed her, his hands shaking with a nervousness and suppressed violence. Then he kissed her mouth, neck and throat; chest and sucked at her breasts, he bit her too hard and she gave a whimper, then he calmed himself, sucking biting and stroking them, each at a time. She held his penis firmly in her hands working her fingers on the head of it, then squeezed the bottom of it, the foreskin rising up and down, paining him. Then he rolled on top of her, she now nibbling discreetly at his ear lobes, flicked her tongue inside his ear and he felt a stabbing erotic heat seized both his brain and penis. She now held it in her hand and placed it on her womb into which he came stabbing like a wild animal; she steadied him with both her arms on his back, her fingers spread gently on them, squeezing him to tell him not so fast, but he plunged plunged, feeling the soft crevices of her, the wet enveloping juices that engulfed his penis, plunging recklessly maddeningly, he bawled out as he felt a suffocating pain stabbed him, coming and plunging in her, she moving slowly from side to side to try and ease the pain, as he rose and thrust himself into her, she moved to the right or left and his penis went into the deepest part of her womb. He came and did not know, his body young powerful energetic, he moved and plunged, moved, plunged, raised it to the top of her and then plunged in like a wild mad man, fighting both her and himself . . . He must have come at least three times in the half hour he was in her, feeling something burning burning at the tip of his penis, giving him pain and torture, but he did not care, until now exhausted and his penis losing its strength involuntarily, mechanically, he ceased like a person suddenly struck by an unnamed sickness. He breathed hard, panted like a dog, surprised to hear the loudness that emerged from his own voice. Cherri laid there covering him with her arms, aware of his strength and power. He rested on her for a brief time, then rolled himself off and curled up like a baby with his back to her. He was curled up like this when he awoke next morning, the sheets showing blood-stains, his own from the forced foreskin. When he tried to pee it burnt and stung him and he washed it in cold water, feeling strong, powerful and baptised.

They slept with each other, seeking in each other solace, comfort and understanding; in each other's arms the world melted away, it was a devouring giant that could not touch their lives, as they pushed the world further away from them, and simultaneously came closer to each other, they felt more than man-woman bondedness, they were like that first night when they slept curled up in each other's arms, brother and sister. And as such they unfolded the dramas of their lives, Cherri, with precaution and timing instructing Michael about what to do to please her. Once he had overcome his initial shyness, he began to express a tenderness and caring for her. At times another world, outside, imposing, influential, told him that he was being sloppy, childish and unmanly, but the feeling of oneness was a concrete bond that could not break, could not fall down or tear away. It made him feel better, and Cherri was beginning to influence to fruition thoughts that he had already conceived, but feared to execute. Mainly, the idea of returning to school. He even volunteered his own age, and she was, in fact, nineteen, three years older than he, but age was immaterial, because their shared feelings transcended those conservative boundaries.

After Roberta had left, Michael sat thinking. His room was put together well, but that was partly Cherri's prompting, not that he was untidy, but the room did not have a certain order, the pieces of furniture were not symetrically aligned to taste. They were just hovering in places without thought of design or order. And she helped him make use of the limited space that he had, the room taking on a feeling of spaciousness, airiness and smiling presentation. Tubbs showed a great deal of admiration for it when he visited him, played dominoes with him or smoked with him. Tubbs was his brother, only different parents sired them, brought them into the world.

A book in his hand, he sat on the bed reading/thinking, when the key began to turn in the lock. He quickly went under the bed, and when Cherri did not find him there, she looked disappointed. She walked up and down the room, looking at where he normally left notes for her, but there was none, and she whispered under her breath, "That damn Rough Black"! She sat on the side of the bed looking into the mirror opposite, looking at the face that stared back at her and wondering desultorily, at her looks, the fact that she would be twenty next year, the thought that she did not look older, maybe not visually, but an inner growth of experience, a tangible transformation of years through accumulated experiences, the twist of her lip of the right side, the small scar on the tip of her right ear that she obtained when she was five in Guyana, the moles on her eyebrow and middle of her bottom lip, and the birthmark on her right cheek that her mother said she got when she was having her and she had a passion for pork and fingered her own face, a tale she never believed, but it never ceased to stay in her mind despite the doctor's explanation of a drop of melanin. These thoughts entered and flew through her mind in this blank space of instant recall, undue mental provocation and the . . . something touched her leg, she did not pay it mind, but it touched her leg again and she stamped her feet, then it touched it again, creepy/crawly, and she stamped her feet and jumped on the bed, a sound of fright emerging from her soft tender lips, and before she could think a rational/logical thought in her provoked state, a hand reached out from under the bed and she screamed!

"Michael, you horrible monster, you dirty dog, you stinking rotten fish, you you you barbarian monster, you unclean piece of pork! Aaaaahhhhh, you! Come out of there". Laughter preceded his body, voluptuous, stinging, biting laughter, mockingly rude, and Cherri pretended to be insulted, pounding him with her fists, pulling his hair and biting him. The bite was painful but sexy and he laughed, throwing himself on the bed. When she sat on his back, silently, like a dog catching a thief and obeying its master's instructions, she just sat there saying nothing, until Michael's convulsion came to a gradual diminishing close. "You need a ten year old sister to play with". Cherri now said, not moving. Michael thought about throwing her off, but he didn't, he liked the smell of her, that Indian scent she always wore, all the natural scents from the earth and trees, she once told him.

"I ought to throw you to the bloody hounds", he said. One way to get her off he thought, would be to tell her about Roberta's visit. "Do you know what? My sister Roberta was here today".

"Liar"!

"Honest, she was. Look at those presents on the chest". She got off instantly and walked over, he turned and sat up. She looked at all the gifts, glad that they were making it up.

"You lucky devil", she cried, "your girlfriend gave this to you and you're telling me about your sister"! Michael laughed.

"Well, you're right about that. Roberta is my girlfriend . . ." Cherri threw a sock at him and he caught it.

"She is, is she? Well, I'm going", she pretended to be walking away.

"You know that you are the one for me, that, everyone can see", he sung these lines, a song by a local band, Brimstone, and she laughed. He could not have imagined that he would have behaved like this a month ago, that his emotion would be capable of this type of performance, without embarrassment. But here, now, in this room, he was bringing strange hidden feelings out of himself, without fear of being seen to be boyish.

"It's really nice of her".

"It was my mother really who sent it. But I'm sure Roberta must have chose them or put something towards it".

"Well, it was very nice".

"And she's getting engaged to a Trinidadian feller name William".

"Do you know him"?

"Yeah. He's OK. A man she deserves".

"Hhmm hhmm", she cleared her throat, "you don't say! Aren't we . . ."

"And she invited me to the party . . ."

"And what did you say, Mr. difficult-to-handle"?

"I said if a couple of my friends could come, I'll come".

"And what did she say".

"She said, yeah, it was OK, yeah".

"I'm glald you're seeing them again after so long, and that they are seeing you too. It should be a good reunion. The prodigal son returns . . ."!

"Well, me an you, an Tubbs an Levi will go".

"Yeah, that should be quite something, me a-tell yo"! They both laughed at her attempt at Roots language. When she spoke the Roots words using her normal intonation and accent, it sounded authentic, but when she tried to speak with that other accent, it produced laughter. She knew it, but did it to make him laugh. Also, it was an imitation of his own speech. Imperceptibly, her own accent was changing, but only slightly. She was a committed Rasta sister, not even eating meat, but Michael felt an unease with her at times, like a hidden aspect of her that he could not reach or understand, and he never probed. Whenever the conversation centred on whites, she became perceptibly heated, vituperous, vindictive, malicious and full of hatred. She would forgive nothing and would concede nothing. Michael, on the other hand though a Rasta, could still relate to whites without fear or apprehension, except the police. It was this that disturbed him, it was this, he thought, that was responsible for the look of intensity and anguish and an almost fanaticism that she carried on her face, and which he had noticed visibly when he had first met her. She was very distant from people in general, but when she made friends, she was dependent and reliable, and gave generously. When Michael had discovered that she was studying to be a teacher, he was a little cowed by their intellectual distance, but she was aware that he held promise, that what he read he digested, that he could speak on what he understood, and could reason on what he was trying to grasp and understand.

This bonded them together, this thirst for knowledge and understanding, this mutual respect for the printed word and its relation to real life in the streets or in history. Beyond that their common sexual compatibility, their mutual tenderness to each other without feeling sissified or punkish, this was their strength and rock. This made the world bearable and less painful, because all the shit was reduced to outside phenomena, external paraphenalia, Cherri's definitions. They read together, discussed together, and hardly quarrelled, except when Michael interpreted some of her actions to be middle-class or white, her attention to detail and to definning things, or approaching things in a particular way. This precipitated his short-termperdness, but simultaneously, he was learning and inculcating her ways. The month that they were together seemed like a year. They were always together.

The party was already well underway when they arrived after 10.30 that Saturday night. When he rang the bell an apprehension gripped his face, Cherri pinched him hard and he almost winced. Tubbs and Levi were standing behind them, and his little sister Eve answered the door and shouted "Mike"! She jumped straight into his arms and he lifted her up, walked through the door and put her down. She raced back inside, flying into the living-room, shouting "Mike is here! Mike is here! He's here with his friends"! He came into the living-room, Funk music was playing, everybody seemed to be jovial and slightly drunk. Before he could say anything, Josie held both his hands, removed his coat and was saying to the room and to herself, "O God, look at the boy nah, look at the boy nah!

Ronnie, you see yuh son, yuh see how yuh son getting big man. O God, look at the boy. Eh eh, he looking good, man. Come in children, come in, take your coats off. Come come, have something to drink first". Michael felt embarrassed by this attention and exposure, but at the same time, he felt triumphant. They thought he would go to the dogs, but here he was looking well, dressed clean. He was wearing jeans and red checked shirt with a brown bomber jacket and expensive shoes. Tubbs was more conservatively dressed: black drain-pipes, brown shirt with brown tie and brown jacket, with his red, gold and green tam on. Both Levi and Cherri were dressed in long Afrikan skirts and blouses, with big earrings, head wrap, shoulder wrap, bracelets and leather bangle. Their skins glistened and shone when they removed their coats, their faces beautiful and natural and radiated dignity and pride. Roberta, for the first time in her life felt a deep pang of jealousy and discomfort for these Rasta sisters. She looked at William eyeing the girls and felt like slapping him. Levi and Cherri looked like sisters or cousins, but Tubbs and Michael were far apart, both in appearance and dress. Tubbs was short, stockily built and heavy, whilst Michael was tall and slim and dressed more contemporaneously.

Ronald came up to Michael and shook his hand, then placed his hand on his shoulder, squeezing it, still holding his hand with the other one. Then he shook Tubbs' hand and said hello to the sisters. Once he had done that, the tension in the room faded away, all was forgiven, but Michael hadn't forgotten. "What you all drinking, or you don't drink"?

"A guinness. We would have a guinness".

"We could handle that. John, bring some guinness dey for your big brother. You sure all you ain want something stronger, eh"?

"Nah. That be alright". The music was wailing, and some kids were dancing self-consciously, aware that people were in the room.

"Well, boy", Ronald said, "I could only say you fooled me. You looking real good. This your girlfriend"? pointing to Levi. Michael nodded his head. Then he took Cherri's hands in his and shook it. "What's yuh name"?

"Cherri", she said, briefly smiling.

"That's a nice name. And what's yours"?

"Levi".

"Unusual name. Sounds like a boy's name. What kind of name is that".

"You can call me Miranda if you like. My parents call me Miranda".

"Well, I could call you Levi if you want. It's not hard to remember, but it's just unusual, that's all. What does it mean".

"It means I born in June, like the sign of the month. Gemini".

"Oho", he said, and John returned with the drinks. Michael was already taking Tubbs around introducing him to his family, cousins, uncles and William. Then two of the younger ones got up and motioned to Michael and Tubbs to sit. They sat and John gave them the guinness. Ronald then asked John to bring in some more chairs from the kitchen for Levi and Cherri. Josie was talking to a woman friend, telling her the whole story about Michael leaving home, turning Rasta, not wanting to go to shcool, arguments with his father, etc. Roberta was trying to attract her mother's eyes to tell her to cool it. Josie saw her, but ignored her signs. She was proud to tell the story, because, surprisingly, her son didn't turn out to be a hooligan. The woman listened with patience, a perpetual smile on her face. The music turned to a Soul ballad, an album playing, one of the latest groups from America. Must be Roberta's records, Michael thought.

Then Josie got up, amidst the talk, the loud music, and stood next to Roberta, "Put on some good calypso nah, Roberta. Ley me and your father have a dance for you gal". William put on a sheepish smile that spilled over into his throat to produce a little chuckle. Roberta made an effort to get up, but William touched her, and he rose to put a record on. He looked through the pile and picked up Kitchener's "Sugar Bum Bum", faded the Funk record out and placed it on the turntable. He turned the volume up loud and as the music started, Josie shouted "O God! Record, boy"! She danced over to Ronnie, put her arms around his waist and they started dancing. Josie moved her huge voluptuous hips, shook them, turned them, while Ronnie's dance was more subdued. William took Roberta's hand and they came on the floor. They danced a break-away, apart from each other, wining their waists cruelly, tantalisingly teasingly sensual. Evelyn got up, and Sam followed her, then Michael got up and took Levi onto the floor. When Michael hit the floor, the dance came back to him instinctively, and he started to move his waist, but Levi had a little difficulty because her background was strictly Reggae, but she still danced beautifully. One of Michael's uncles got up and held Josie's friend's hands and brought her onto the floor protesting, but when she began to dance, all hell broke loose. The woman went down on the floor shaking her waist, got up and made some bold hip-shaking pumping sexual movements, her fat breasts dangling in the air like a mad-bull (a big kite), ducking up and down. Tubbs sat watching, but Cherri raised him up. He started saying "No no no", but she held him and they danced. Once the collective spirit held him, he was part of the community, the tribal flow, the ebb of the dangerous movement of tide, rushing up and down the shore. Tubbs clapped his hands, shook his head, moved his feet, and watched the outlandish woman, and began to imitate her hip-movements. The whole room came alive and people were singing along, "Sugar Bum, Sugar Bum Bum, Sugar Bum, Sugar Bum Bum", but Josie went further and was singing along with the verses. The record was long, and brought perspiration and exhilaration to the minds and bodies of the tribe. Before the track had finished, William had mischeviously selected another tune that would rip them apart, "Rasta Man" by Lord Melody. When the tribe heard this, they went mad. Even conservative Tubbs, hearing this song about Rasta, loosened his tie, threw his jacket on the chair and wailed with the tribe, up and down the floor he danced, throwing his hands into the air, and singing "Rasta Man, Rasta Man, be careful"! along with everybody. They had changed partners, and Cherri went and held onto Michael who was himself wailing, and Levi danced wherever Tubbs danced. Happiness, exhilaration, released tensions, energetic magnetism, all passed through their minds. Tubbs thought his body couldn't take any more, but William had already put on Merchant's "Um-Ba-Yo". When Tubbs heard the words "Afrika" and "Warrior" he flung himself into the music like a mad man, jumping into the air with his hands outstretched, reaching for some invisible power in the sky. Levi was herself shocked, never having seen him in a spirit like this, but loved it, throwing herself with more vigour and spirit into the dance. Josie's friend was down on the ground again, turning her waist like an axis, the uncle throwing dog-jucks at her in imitation of the sexual act itself. Roberta, William, Josie and Ronald saw this battle and crowded round the couple, laughing, clapping and pushing them to greater heights. When they realised that they were the center of attraction the woman broke away, pummelling her waist at her partner like she was withdrawing from him every ounce of his sexuality, every juck of her waist, violent, crude, controlled and dangerous, brought about a deeper response from uncle. They fought this battle with relentless vigour and violence, each one outdoing every feat that was previously achieved, egging each other on, hot, sweaty, energised, they literally sucked each other's vital parts, smashing them, renewing them, bringing them to erection and incredulity. Tubbs, Cherri and Levi had never seen anything like this before. They stared dumbfounded, aghast, petrified, but full of admiration, the lack of loss of Afrikan culture, the perpetuation of a tradition that they felt only Rastas had carried on. But this act, this partnership, had proven that the *cultural* traditions of Afrikans were unbroken, but the education is what had destroyed us. He, like both Levi and Cherri, felt a kind of contempt, a hidden part of themselves, suppressed, pressed to the bottom of their souls, stagnated and prevented from rising up like the inevitable vomit, was being reflected, expressed and exhibited.

When the record had come to an end, they grabbed uncle and the woman, shook their hands, raised them in the air, patted them on their backs, congratulated them, and showered them with drinks. The woman was now visibly tired and said so. Probably, this was the first time in years that she had behaved this way. She held uncle's hand and shook it. They squeezed each other's hands communicating to each other how good they were, and what they were still capable of. Josie brought out paper towels for them to wipe their hot sweaty bodies. William changed the music to a Lover's Rock, Louisa Mark, which sent everybody cuddling their partners. This quieted the loud voices and laughter, and stillness and thought brought the room back to sanity. The music was soft and authoritative, bringing to the world of dancers the idea of romance and love. When Louisa Mark hit the high notes, it brought a feeling of pain, passion and longing in the hearts of the young couple, bringing them closer to themselves, understanding the need to be closely knitted together, to be one emotionally and as a group or community.

Later in the night, with everybody high or drunk, somebody started shouting "Speech, speech", as Ronald tried to make a discreet exit to the kitchen. Josie's woman friend said, "Don't run away, Ronnie, you're the girl fadder, why you ain say a few words, eh"? Josie grabbed Ronald round the waist laughing, "Yeh, Ronnie, you suppose to bless the children engagement by saying a few words". Ronnie now felt cornered and could not escape. A record was playing and William turned down the volume, hiding at the back, saying "Speech, speech". Ronnie then decided he had better say a few words. Josie brought him to the middle of the room.

"Just a minute, ladies and gentlemen", he said, waving his hands in the air for quiet, "I don't know what you want me to say, but . . ."

"Just say something", a voice said.

"No heckling tonight, eh, let me finish . . ."

"Let the man talk", Josie said, her face scowling.

"Yes, as I was saying, I don't know what you expect me to say, as her father I am very proud of my daughter. She is, as we say, the apple of my eye, a man's daughter always is, especially a first chile". They clapped. "Quiet, let me finish, let me finish. I'm not a good talker, I'm not good with words. I'm not, what de man name", he turned to Roberta, "the writer feller . . ."

"George Lamming"?

"No. The Guyanese writer who write "To Sir With Love", what's his name"?

"Braithwaite, E.R. Braithwaite", Michael volunteered. Everybody looked at him with astonishment, Roberta shooting a quick glance at him, and Josie putting her hand to her mouth.

"Yes. That's the man. I'm no E.R. Braithwaite with words, but I can say that my Roberta is a good girl and would make any good man a damn happy man". Applause and laughter. "And any man doubt that is a damn liar"! Applause and laughter. Roberta was beginning to feel distinctly embarrassed, but when her father was in this mood, she felt she had better not say anything because he would say more. This mood was rare. "Yes, as I was saying. Roberta is a damn good girl, and William, I'm sorry his parents wasn't here tonight, but they have brought up a gentleman". Applause. "From what I see of him, and that's not much"! Applause and laughter. William clapped and laughed heartily. "But birds of a feather flock together, and what better pair of birds can you get, eh". Applause and pats on the back. Then someone shouted, "A toast to their future". Michael and Tubbs went around pouring into glasses and they toasted to their future, wishing them happiness and a quick marriage. They drank, music played and people danced and enjoyed themselves. Before the evening came to a close uncle and Josie's friend had their arms around each other, and the close-knit family members knew that ole uncle had scored again.

They all came to Michael's room. It was 5 a.m. when they had reached home. Ronnie had driven them although he was very drunk. But Michael knew that even in his drunkenness, he showed a remarkable alertness and caution. He shook all their hands, even kissing Cherri and Levi, something Michael had never seen him do, drunk or sober, to anybody outside his daughters. He couldn't believe this was his father, the same man who had argued with and troubled him so much. When they reached the room, they quickly took off their shoes and lit the paraffin heater and Michael took the small two-bar electric heater from under the bed and plugged it in. Then Tubbs took out some ganja and between them rolled three joints. Michael took a mattress from off the bed and put it on the floor, Cherri bringing out some old sheets she had given to Michael. She made the bed and they paired off into twos: Cherri and Levi, Tubbs and Michael sitting on each bed, talking about the events of the night and smoking. Michael brought out his cassette player and played some Al Campbell music, soft and sedate, that he had previously taped.

It was seven o'clock when they finally went to bed, the parrafin heater burning, its wick flickering a bright blue/yellow, a symbol, perhaps of the night and the rising day.

7

REASONINGS & PARTINGS OF WAYS

It was now over six months since Michael held down the job. He had accomplished much more than he planned, but the thought of the money he collected had also played on his mind. Already, having met Ron, the white boy, in the amusement arcade, he was ing met Ron, the white boy, in the amusement arcade, he was beginning to bring home bits of cloth and clothes. He would give them to his fence, in this case Nose or Stabber, and they would get rid of them. He paid them a commission, but Nose in particular always insisted that Michael called his own price and he would sell in requirement of his own profit. Almost every week for the last ten weeks he was bringing home something. The extra money he made didn't go on herb, but in a savings account at the National Westminister Bank, not where he lived or worked, but in Notting Hill. This way, he figured, if he was ever caught, they would never discover that he had any savings.

His talks with Cherri about the best course to take for his education was practical, rather than motivating. He had already made his mind up. In another three months he would attend college full-time taking GCE at oridinary level, if he failed miserably, he told himself, college was out. But Cherri was smart, she never tried to teach him anything, and waited until he had approached her. Every other evening, she gave him lessons in English, Maths, History, and so on. Maths he was tops in, but English he had to relearn what he had previously learnt and History, he thought, was boring because he hated learning about white people. But she was a good teacher. They also discussed his plan to steal the money he collected from Mrs. Appleton. Cherri didn't approve (but didn't say so), not because she disapproved of sealing, but because she did not want to risk him putting his neck under the guillotine. She wanted him to continue to warm and bring joy into her life.

At work, Mrs Appleton was suffering from some kind of sickness. It wasn't a cold or her heart or some sickness that you could put your finger on. It was something to do with "woman business". This he had heard the little old ladies discussing during their lunch breaks. Having nothing better to do, they discussed every little phenomenon that appeared out of the ordinary. Yes, they were saying, Mrs Appleton didn't look well at all. Sometimes she complained of her sight, headaches, backache or bellyache, but there was no remedy in medicines. She just suffered. Michael didn't know if to feel sorry for her or not, but he did pay attention to her illness, offering to do anything she wanted him to. She was beginning to rely upon him even more. She was allowing him to handle bigger and bigger collections. The time was drawing near, he thought, I already have the new room in Hammersmith, that's far away enough from Harlesden. When they come to my address, I won't be there. I would just lie low for two or three months, then hit the streets again. He had no furniture to move out of the room, because it was furnished. Only his personal belongings and those weren't too many. He moved these to the new room which was much better in space and decoration than the previous one. In fact it was Cherri who had gotten it for him. She knew a friend who was attending the training college with her – a white girl in fact – and she was getting a job as a teacher in South London and thought the distance too far to commute. So Michael got it. The rent was £9.50. It was mainly white tenants, Cherri told him, but it was a huge house and people, mostly young studentish white, minded their own business. The landlord didn't live on the premises either, so any illusions of personal hassles would be absent. He liked the area, it was close to the tube, buses, and the street was clean, there was even a green farther down his street where kids played football, netball and lawn tennis.

He was to visit three customers who were paying him cash. He went and made Mrs Appleton a cup of coffee and had brought her in some danish rolls that she liked so much. She blew her nose, thanked him, gave him £2, and sent him off, saying there wasn't much to do, so he could take his time. As he walked out the ladies smiled at him, he smiled back knowingly. He left and unhurriedly collected nearly £500. He took the bus to his new place and played some records, fixed himself a sandwich and relaxed. Mrs. Appleton was beginning to get worried when she saw it was 4 p.m. and Michael hadn't returned. She got red, her face glowing like an UFO, paced the floor, wiped her face, fixed her black dress, put her hands through her hair a dozen times, looked at both her watch and the company clock, and grew distraught and tearful. The little old dears were looking at her, working, looking at her. At quarter to five, she told them the whole story. They all looked shocked, opened their mouths wide, and said he must have fallen sick. She didn't call the police, thinking that they were perhaps correct. But the next day there was no Michael, no telephone call, no visit from a stranger with a note. She thought about calling in the police, but delayed it. The old dears were sympathetic and understanding, but privately they gossiped amongst themselves that they knew he was no good, that he was too good to be true, that he had them fooled, and oh poor Mrs Appleton now going through such a bad period in her life, what with her menopause and all that.

The same night Cherri visited him and she questioned everything that he did that day. She felt positive that he had acted correctly, but there was a nagging doubt in her mind . . . The next day he deposited £100 at the bank and gave the other £400 to Cherri to keep. That was their plan. Michael hardly went out after that. Out of the money he had made selling clothes he paid six weeks rent in advance and had enough food for over a week in stock. He spent his days reading, going to the library, reading the newspapers and taking out books, and going over the work he was doing with Cherri. Cherri wanted to be with him every day, but she forced herself to stay at home every odd night because she had her own studies to do, her own papers to write. There was a pay phone in the hall where he now lived and Cherri rang him each night that she stayed home. It was always at the same time: eight o'clock. Sometimes she would bring cooked food for him. He never felt scared or immoral about what he had done. To expect a human being to be stooping, to be submissive and without thought to himself, he felt, was to expect the impossible. Such a person, he believed, deserved the worst.

He had a great deal of time to think and meditate upon what he wanted to do and be. The sound system idea still held his interest, but he now realised that on its own it could never satisfy him. But he still loved to follow the sound man, to participate in the tribal act of lifting boxes, loading the truck, unloading and wiring up the boxes, turntable and amp. The best part was his playing, but even that wasn't as regular as it used to be. He thought it was strange that he was not having any dreams of him playing to an audience, and conquering them. Now he had few dreams, and those that came into his head were how to make his life better, how to get on and still be himself. Sometimes he would listen to the radio, the discussions, political and otherwise, the slant of announcers late at night when they discussed the "immigrant" question. He would cuss loudly and call them racist bastards. Sometimes his violence would rise in him and he would turn the radio off. But he, nevertheless, enjoyed these discussions, if only because it made him aware of what the white world was thinking.

It was July and the summer now looked as it was supposed to be, warm, bright blue skies and people in their shirt-sleeves. The papers were full of coverage of the National Front, and when he visited the Community Centre he would hear the older brothers discuss the workings of the NF and that they believed that it must be in existence because they were being funded both by big business and some politicians. Even the Marxist brothers couldn't dispute this. They also felt that if there wasn't a real connection with the police and the NF officially, the ordinary rank and file of the police force were on the side of the NF. They drew the reference to the fact that police are provided to "protect" the NF from opposition groups when they marched. And that when the Anti-Nazi League and the Rock Against Racism mob demonstrated, the police did not escort them, did not protect them from violent attacks, but in fact joined the attack. There was talk that the NF was considering marching through the Ladbroke Grove area. This was drawn from the fact that some Asian butchers had their shop-fronts smashed in and spray-painted with racialist propaganda.

The idea of walking with or at least keeping a dangerous weapon entered his mind then. He went home that afternoon and wrapped a piece of hollow pipe with red tape so that it looked like a stick or piece of wood. The idea of a knife had entered his mind, but he thought better of it because he could be stopped at random and searched or picked up for SUS. The taped pipe could be easily camouflaged and he could probably invent a reason for walking with it on the spot. He couldn't think of an instant story, but it was less likely that he would be charged with being in possession of a deadly weapon or intent to do injury.

Cherri had spoken to her father about Michael, but not in a direct way (I have a friend, dad), and asked whether he might know of any jobs that were going. He took some time, thought about it, and said that a musician friend of his was in the removal business by day and worked as a professional musician at night. This pleased her, and it made her father curious. In fact he now noticed that over the past few months a twinkle had entered her eye, she seemed more at ease, more contented, and that when she did spend time away from home she stayed out for a long time. He didn't say anything, but just asked casually who was this "friend"? "O", she said after some hesitation, "a Rasta friend of mine. He's not working right now". "Oh", he said, "I see". That was all that was said.

Michael got the number from Cherri. He rang up and the man asked him to come over. He went over, the man "interviewed" him, asked him where he was working previously, for how long, how much money he made, and why he left. He thought all of this would come up, so he told him that he hadn't worked for four months and that his previous job was working in a record shop but that the shop closed up. Bennett (that was his name) believed him, even sympathised, saying that he knew the record business wasn't a sound one and that business fluctuated, etc. A nice man, Michael thought. Bennett took him on, that same day he went out on a job. He had to travel with Bennett in a ford transit van all the way over to Brixton. They went up three flights of rickety stairs that creaked and looked dangerous. An old black woman lived on the second floor, the door unlocked and as they knocked, she shouted for them to come in, she, making last minute adjustments to her packing. The woman looked wrinkled, with a large birthmark that covered half of her face. She had thin straight hair, a mixture of grey/black, as though she had Indian in her. She talked with a business chop, and motioned a lot with her bony arms. Michael was already laughing inside.

"Mr Bennett, I hate moving. Oh, its a cruelty of life, but you have to, you know, you have to. I've been in this house for twenty-eight years, since the time I first came to this country, and I've lived here ever since. The whites used to live here, what we called the petty middle-class, some of them, some were just workers, drunks. Oh, we had a lot of them, the Irish too, yes. Fights, I tell you, right out there", she said, pointing a small finger, a marriage ring showing on the next hand, "you won't believe that, would you. Take the trunks down first. Don't worry about those wardrobes, these new Council houses have built-in wardrobes, I saw them. Lovely. Around here was lovely then, back in those days. Yes, you would never believe that, would you. Twenty-eight years ago, this house was beautiful, but as the West Indians moved in, the whites ran out. The smart Jewish landlords bought out the houses and in those days if you had money you could buy this house for a £1000, yes, a £1000. But West Indians couldn't even afford that. I used to work for £4.50 a week in those days. You could do a lot with that in those days, not now, not now . . . I have four of those trunks for you to move Mr. Bennett, the rest is old furniture, but I've grown accustomed to those things. My friends tell me I should throw them away, nobody would buy that today, they said. I said, throw them away! They're antique, they could fetch a good penny in the antique market. That stopped them dead in their tracks. But you know, those aren't antique. Nah. They're just old furniture, I only said that to stop the talk about modern furniture. Junk, junk! They have no style . . ." Bennett and Michael were lining up the trunks, bringing them to the door, while she talked. When they had lined them up, they started taking them down, one by one. Even when they were already half way down the stairs, they could hear her voice. "Sell my furniture, they must be joking! That modern stuff is junk, these are Victorian, even if faked Victorian, ha ha ha ha . . ." she chortled at the doorway.

Every bit of her furniture fitted perfectly into the van. It was a single trip job, Michael sitting in the back with the furniture, while the old lady sat with Bennett at the front. She was talking about the height of the van and comparing it to a bus. She liked it, the feel was nice, it made you see people different. And, ah, she pointed out the various places that were being torn down: this used to be a pub, this used to be a fish & chips place, now its a Kentucky Fried, etc., now, mind you, she never liked fish & chips, but chicken, especially made by the Americans . . . She talked all the way to Blackheat. The Council buildings seemed very decent, Michael thought. They were only four stories high and she was on the second floor, but there was no lift. She told them she had had a good look at the place, that she had refused to move eight times before, over the last five years. Shit houses, she said they were, piss and shit, and nasty children, no manners, she said, black and white, she said, all filthy and unmannerly. No, she would never take a place like that. Patience is a virtue, the race is not for the swift, etc . . .

The old lady peeled off £30 for Bennett, but he only accepted £20. She was beginning to protest, "No, Mr. Bennett, I never accept charity. I always pay my way". Bennett told her that he had miscalculated, that the figure he had given her was based on two trips, but since they made it in one, the price was lower. Michael felt that he was lying. "Oh, alright. £20 is your charge and £10 is my tip. Thank you very much Mr. Bennett, and that young feller too. God bless you both". Bennett couldn't argue against such diplomacy and brightness. He simply patted the old woman's arm and wished her the best. She took his number again, saying that she might need him to do something for her, or her friends might, you never can tell. Bennett gave it to her and they left.

The next job was in Hornsey. That too was easy, there was not much furniture. That was also the last job for the day. They had only been on the road for five hours altogether. Michael enjoyed the work because new people were always coming into view. Bennett was a character as well. He talked about sex and women, his favourite subjects, it seemed. But he could also get worked up about politics or the state of the nation just as quickly. The way in which he saw the society was compartmentalised. He believed that the wholeness of a society, nation or race, that people spoke about was an illusion. It was an illusion, he said, precisely because the small group which wielded power wanted to keep the people divided. So, he believed that there would never be any substantial change in the world, i.e., the world would never change morally because greed and the need to promote self or better the individual was stronger than the collective good. If a man was drowning he said, he would literally grab at a straw. And if two men were drowning they would both fight over the same straw. None would survive anyway. Thus he felt that any political movement that spoke of change was principally speaking about change for that particular political movement and their friends. He said there was no difference between the European ruling the Caribbean and Afrika and the black man ruling those same areas. In both instances the majority of the people suffered and the minority prospered. Once Bennett got talking he could never stop. He even drew references to how musicians functioned in a band. The band may have a set arrangement, but the individual musician would want to rise above the rest by playing more on his instrument. Thus he robs the band of the promised unity of arrangement and discipline. He believed that man was an animal and the only thing that suppressed his animalism was religion, but it was being exploited by its leaders. The leaders would reap the financial or sexual benefits, but the flock would remain loyal to the idea. So even in religious matters man was at conflict. There was no solution for the human race, he believed, none!

Michael listened to him rant and rave, agreeing with most or all that he had said, but when he reached home and thought about it, he thought Bennett had most of it right, but something nagged, scratched and tumbled at the bottom of his stomach . . . Instead of working it out comprehensively, cohesively, he only had confusion. Bennett was deep, he felt, but his personal experiences must have led him to these conclusions. He couldn't say anything to rebut what Bennett had said. There was nothing in his own experience to test what Bennett had so dramatically expounded. The way he talked was so powerful, authoritative and stylish that anybody would believe him. Generous guy though, Michael thought, he bought me lunch.

Cherri came over that evening. She couldn't hide the excitement on her face, she wanted to know everything, about the man, about the job, and what it was all about. Michael laughed before he could start. She was just like Roberta. He told her the story. She asked questions about the old woman, but he couldn't answer because he didn't know. The second client was a black woman and her son. She asked questions about this too.

"So what do you think then"?

"Oh, its awright, you know. I think it's OK. It don't demand too much".

"Yeah. But dad did say that Bennett was a bit of a gabber. Did he bore you then"?

"Nah. I told you that Bennett is awright, really. He talks a lot, but like he thinks, you know. Like he's made a study of people, nothin gets past his eyes. He's a bright feller. But the way he goes on about sex and women you would think he's a bloody maniac. But when he talked about politics, it was the same enthusiasm, really. O, he's a nut. The work is cool. I won't knock it. But I'm hungry. You gonna cook some food then"?

"Yeh dread, yuh know. One minute its talk, next minute its food. The man well love him belly, you see! Oooohhhh"! It was the first time that he recognized a trace of a Guyanese accent in her, and this tickled him.

"After talk is food", he said with an accent, already putting his hands up to protect himself. She looked at him with a broad smile, her whole face lighting up, put her hands on her hips and laughed.

"Alright, Mr. Blumenthal, we'll see who eats today. I know what a good cook you are". She laughed again.

"I was only joking", he said in a child's voice, shaking his head.

"Then tell mummy you're sorry then. Go on, like a good obedient child".

"I'm sorry mummy, baby's sorry". He made up his face like a crying sorrowful baby, and she placed her hand on his head. They both had a good laugh and she cuddled and kissed him, getting romantic.

"I ain ask for all of that", pushing her away, "all I want is some food, woman. Cook the I some bloodclaath food! I man want eat"! She got up laughing and went to the kitchen. The house wasn't converted, so the kitchen was shared. Actually, they imagined that since it was whites living in the l ouse the kitchen would have been in a state, but it was rigorously kept clean because the three tenants who lived and shared the ground floor space (including Michael) devised a rota system. Nobody gave trouble. This was one myth that he saw went up in flames. The cooker was always well cleaned and the kitchen nearly spotless.

The doorbell rang. He answered it. It was Nose and Stabber. They hailed each other, came into the room and sat down.

"Yeh hear about them bloodclaath National Front, Rough Black"?

"Nah, wha happen"?

"Bwoy", Stabber said, "them want march through Ladbroke Grove. Them white man want we fe lick them bloodclaath or wha"!

"Bwoy", Nose said, "if dem bring dem bomberclaath come say dem marching through de Grove, dem go be sorry".

"How you heard this, man"?

"We just come from de Grove looking for some herb, man, and hear dem man dey talking bout it. Man, it go be one wicked killing for dem bloodclaath". Stabber was fuming, as though the fight was already on in his mind.

"Yuh heard wha dem man do in Ladbroke Grove? Dem smash up some Paki business and paint fockery on de walls. Bwoy, dem man looking fe a licking". Nose apprehended the act like a declaration of war, an insult, even though there was apparently no love lost between him and the Asians, a race, he said he despised even more than the white man. It was his favourite hate subject and he always said that the first opportunity he got to fuck a "true true" Asian girl, he would, just to fuck up the father. He actually meant it, and his hatred was vituperative.

"Bwoy, me no love dem Asian man dem, but Jah know di Babylon a wicked."

"Yeah, man", Stabber agreed. "I man doh love dem neither. Dem fuck up, man."

"You know a Asian rather his daughtah marry a white man than a black man?"

"Yeah, man, I man know that. Is wha dem come from? Some likkle poor country wid no bloodclath food, and dem starving and not accustomed to nothin. See when they come here they don't even know how to use a toilet! Dem does wash dem face in the toilet bowl! And when dem shit, dem stand up and they aim miss and go all on di floor. Yeah, man! I man know dat."

"Is true, yes", Michael joined in.

"But look here", Stabber said, "Dis is serious business. Dem man dey doh associate demselves wid blackman, you know. All dem a do is do a business, seen? Yeah, mahn, is just a business dem a deal wid, and dem doh have nothin to offer. Dem really hate blackman. Dem doh have nothin fe do wid blackman except as a bloodclath customer."

"Did the man dem sight the article in the newspaper the other day. One Asian man they interviewed in *The Evening Standard* said the white man come first, then come the Asian, and the black man the lowest of the low." Everybody was talking about that article, and Nose, "He didn't even say that the black man was last, but the lowest of the low". That seemed to profoundly upset him. Sometimes he became so enraged and bitter that he would just go into an Asian store and rip-off two or three shirts just to see if they would try to hold him. It must have been the meanness of his face, his deliberate slowness in theft that frightened the store-keepers. Nobody approached him, but just looked on in horror.

"So what dem man say dem go do"?

"O", Nose said, "is just talk bout a counter demonstration, that when dem walk through the ghetto, dem go walk through as well. That is fockery, man. Black people suppose to defend themselves,to show dem likkle bloodclaath bwoys dem once and for all that is black man dem a deal wid, not no likkle rassclaath coolie bwoy. Rasta, is we a go have fe defend we rights. Is we a go fe show dem that dem cahnt mess with the youth"!

"I man will well defend truths and rights, yo no see it"? Stabber said.

"Is that we a defend yes", Nose confirmed.

"We go have fe do someting yes", Michael also agreed, "but if we doing anyting, it go have fe come from inside de bloodclaath counter demo, yuh see it dey! We inside the counter demo, but ready fe do we tings"!

"Seen", both Nose and Stabber said. The sense of what Michael said came to Nose and Stabber like a wound. It sounded like a workable plan.

"Dem man dey go come armed, you know. Dem National Front people dey, dey well armed, you know. An the police go protect dem too. They will have police surrounding the National Front people and when de attack come dey go jump in", Nose said.

"Yeah", said Stabber, "that is one ting we go have fe look for. Dem police go come well armed with dey weapons, so is two fight we go have fe fight, you no see it? The man dem go have fe come out in force, an walk wid dem tings. Every man go have fe walk wid dem tings, otherwise is slaughter we go get slaughter, an I man no dead for nothin stupid. I man defend I rights but I want fe live, yo no see it? So is weapon we go have fe come out wid to defend weself gainst dem man dey".

"It gon be like war! Prophecy will have to fulfill", Nose said. "Is not gon be like some likkle bloodclaath fight . . . blood a go have fe bloodclaath run! Man go have fe barl an stand up an defend blackman".

"Seen", said Stabber and Michael.

"If dem National Front really come through de Grove, bwoy, this is one bloodclaath they go have to write in the bloodclaath history books", Michael said with aggression and violence.

"An Notting Hill, mi hear mi fadder say, was blood in de 1950s, man. Black man had to run from dem white man dey. When Babylon pass an see black man a get de lick him turn him bloodclaath hypocritical face or walk cross de street an let black man get stab an lick. Notting Hill was in blood! Mi fadder say even dem Irish man was attacking black man in dem times dey. Him a rassclaath immigrant, doing de dirty work fe de Englishman dem, and him a de first to defend the Englishman rights! Ha, dem paddies mad no bloodclaath! Still, is black man a win de victory. Man come from all Brixton to Notting Hill to defend black man rights, an dem white get a bloodclaath licking. But me fadder say dat when de case dem come to court is black man getting bloodclaath jail. De judge say dat dem sympathise wid black man being attacked, but dat is no reason to retaliate wid violence, dat dey should complain to de police an bring de case to court! You ever hear ting so? De Babylon dem defending white man, black man getting stab up, an black man must go fe de police to bring case to bloodclaath court! Dey must tink dat black man stupid an dohn see is defend him a defend white man using him legal profession fe do so. Bwoy, de white man full er bomberclaath tricks"!

They had all heard the story before, but they were not aware of the details of the conflict until Stabber had brought them to light.

The violence and aggression that they individually and collectively felt, experienced and reflected was born out of the limitations, they felt, that were imposed on them by white society. They could not aspire, with any degree of consciousness, to be anything if they were discriminated against and beaten down into withdrawing into themselves. But they had said (over and over again) that they were a new generation of black man, they did not aspire to be part of the Babylonian system that was Britain, that there was nothing the white man could offer them, unless it was freedom! And they will never get that, they all knew, unless it was wrested from them with violence, unless they were beaten into submission. When Tappa Zukie sang about MPLA, the words were not important because the subject-matter was already widespread in the media: TV, radio and the press, but it reinforced the focus on white rule in southern Afrika and the black guerillas fighting for freedom, not around a table, but with guns in their hands. That was the symbol: Violence!

When the sound man played his music and the lyrics talked personally to them about rights, about oppression, about rip-off, about struggle, the music itself took on a power of tremendous resistance, the bass/drums combination stretching the senses to vibrational awareness, to bullets riddling the imagination, to centuries of spirit unfolding in the head, committing them through ancestors, through fallen heroes, to struggle, to fight. And all the trappings of success, all the symbols of the aspiring black man doing good in Babylon, all the gadgets to satisfy oppression, could not make them give up the belief that black man *culture* (the mode and symbols of his dress, walk, hair style, and *speech: it was not that they could not understand the white man – they understood him only too well – but that he could not understand them*) *must be made the strength of his survival*!

They always heard the older brethren say that the white man in Rhodesia for all the centuries that he lived in Afrika, boasted to the TV camera that he was a Rhodesian, still dressed, acted and spoke like an Englishman. It was also true, they said, of white communities in Australia, New Zealand, and all over the world where indigenous populations were decimated as a rational policy. Yet, the brothers said, the Englishman talked about being swamped by blacks, of being undertaken in population by blacks, of having their culture transformed by blacks, and of blacks wanting to keep their way of life, that if they lived in England they must adjust to the culture and history of their host country . . . Haaaaha! The brothers laughed, the Englishman is the most hypocritical animal in Europe. Jordan used to say that if you watched the true Englishman, dressed so stupid in their bowler hat, three piece black suit, their necks locked down with a tie, the proverbial umbrella in their hands, and their flattering insipid voices, you would never believe that such an "honest" "decent" man could rule and control the world so ruthlessly. This produced great raucous and crude laughter amongst them: the image was like the clarity of a memory photographed in space and time, so bluntly real and cruel. It made them see the cleverness, the bile, the snaky method of deception that the Englishman employed to continue to wield and control power.

Michael left the room, went to the kitchen and told Cherri to cook some more food, that Nose and Stabber were here. She either pretended to be hurt or in fact was, but she raised her hand and slapped her thighs and wrinkles came to her brow. She wasn't mad that she was asked to cook more food, but that the food was already cooking, and that she would have to do the process all over again. Michael volunteered to help, and even though she refused, the wrinkles and the scowl were beginning to gradually disappear. He took two onions out and cut them up, he scrubbed the potatoes, not peeling them because they contained their potency in their skins, and washed some more greens, while Cherri picked some more rice and entered the communal fridge for some frozen peas. Internally, she was smiling because even though Michael tried to come over like an orthodox Rasta, she knew that it was part pretense, because he always offered to help and actually did so. When he had completed his contribution, he returned to the room.

Nose and Stabber had already rolled two large spliffs and were drawing heavily. They were silent for a long while, having switched on the small black & white TV, they were watching it, smoking, and looking relaxed. When Nose had finally exhaled, having held the smoke down for a long time as though he wanted his lungs to expand and his brains swell up, Michael asked him if he had a camera to sell.

"I man have a lot er camera, but they go cheap and quick because a lot of people don't want camera. I had one up to yesterday, but I sold it to dis bredder dey, Tony, the black bredder who now dreading".

"What else the man have to sell"?

"O I could get you a good cassette deck for £40, if you want it". As he inhaled and exhaled his voice took on a choked but clear quality. It was almost a style of smoking, talking in a throaty creaking voice that became a cultural stance.

"What kind you got"?

"Right now I have two Sony".

"Yuh tink you can hold one for me"?

"Only for about a week".

"O let me tell you dis", Stabber came in, "me an Nose went to do a job in Bayswater. We didn't have no information bout dis job, right, an it was dark, so we picked the front door lock and went up to the first floor. We stan outside listening to see if anybody inside, you know, the radio or TV, but we hear nothin. So I man take mi knife out an opened the lock, right. So we get inside an find dis nice colour TV an deck, they had nice stereo too but we couldn't take everyting. When we get de tings an put dem outside de door, someting tell de I fe check upstairs. Nose want leave because we have we tings, but I man step back inside an went into another room, an de house was luxurious, mi a tell you, an bloodclaath! when mi push open de door, is two bloodclaath batty men, naked as dey born, fucking each other! HAHAHAHAHAHA! Bwoy, de big fat one had dis little skinny one, the bwoy was maybe sixteen, an him was fucking him in him arse. An when mi open de door dem jump up, but mi pull mi knife an cut de bloodclaath fat one in him batty, mi a tell you! Bloodclaath, I man was laughing as him jump up and start barling for him life. The little bloodclaath skinny one was biting the bomberclaath pillow an was crying like a baby. Stabber come an we both give dem a bloodclaath lick. We even take de TV an deck downstairs an come back fe de rest later. Bwoy, mi a tell you, I man never sight a ting like dat before, and I man hope never".

"The bloodclaath white man stink, man"!

"Yeah", Michael said, "but black man doing de same ting too . . . "

"Wha"! Stabber fumed, "is only because the white man bring him poison pon we people dem. Black man never go on wid dem tings inna Afrika, never. We was warriors, Rasta. But is when slavery happen an we cross dem murderous waters dey, an dem bring we come pon de plantation an have we work like slaves, is den dem have we do tings against we will, an still we fight dem down same way, struggle gainst dem same way. Dat is why you have Maroon an dem man dey, Cuffy an Paul Bogle, an den you have Rasta. Seen. Is white man ting dat, batty fucking".

"An dem Arab too, is pure batty fucking a go on wid dem. Between dem an de white man dem have de world covered. Is pure batty fucking go on wid dem men dey. Black man never take part in dem tings. Den I man hear dem talk about, wha dem talk about, sexual freedom, but is only freedom to fuck a batty, you no see it? If dem so free dem should be dung in a woman pussy, fucking it, but what, dem dohn fuck dem woman, dem have fe turn to woman to get fuck. Is man fucking man, and woman fucking woman".

"Better for we still", Michael added with a smile, beginning to crack his knuckles, "because when dem fuck man, an woman fuck woman, is we who go populate an out number dem. Den is pure controlling dis land".

"Even though dem homosexual, dem na stop being racist, you know. Dem queer up an fuck up, but dem na forget to oppress black man, control black man an brutalise black man. Some of dem bloodclaath get worser! See, the way dem behave wid a black man is either to fuck him or control him. A fucked black man is a dead black man! See dat? See dat? Is either dem fuck him or dem oppress him. I hear some man say dat homosexual understand black man better than de ordinary white man, but dat is pure fuckery! Dem understand who..? Not I, Rasta. Dem dohn understand I a tall. Still, I man dohn want fem fe understand I". Stabber was fuming, his eyes red, his face scowling, his brow creased and wrinkled, his mouth screwed up, violence flaring thru his words, his stance, his demonstrating hands, the power of his convictions. Stabber's emotions flared and flailed the room like reigning terror.

'I man dohn want nothin to do wid no white man", Nose said quietly, resolutely. "Dem dohn have nothin dat I man want". He pounded his chest and scowled. "Dem dohn have a bloodclaath ting right now over I, except dem machinery, dem weapons of violence, but history show I dat de ungodly always bloodclaath fall. De Pope in Rome . . . Rome is a dead place. Earthquake cover up de place, an it go happen again. Dem going dung an dey go go dung more, yo no see it? Spain was great, Portugal was great, running slaves and conquering de bloodclaath Caribs an Arawaks, taking away dem lan, but wha? See dem a bloodclaath fall! Only righteousness reigns. See it dey! The meek will inherit de earth. Dat is I an I".

"Another ting dem come wid is education", Stabber said, now feeling articulate, as though he knew all the solutions, as though, now, the spirit had taken hold of him and clarity of thought and feeling had merged on a pure plane of wisdom... "See when black man fight gainst dem, dem had fe free we up, dem had to leggo. So what dem do? Dem start say, awright, if dem fight we dung so, make dem have some education, make dem understand we culture so dat dem will stop fight we. Seen? So the few likkle bloodclaath house boy dem give education to start behaving like a Englishman. Seen? An right now! Right now here", he said dramatically, pointing to the floor, "dem still a fool we wid dem education. Seen? If a man know a ting bout architecture, or medicine or science, dem man dey suppose to help him black bredder. Seen? Bo no! Dem education mash dem up, dem education educate dem to tek from we what we ain have. Seen? We ain have money, so dem form political party to exploit we, vote for dem, put dem in power, an den make dem bloodclaath rich. Seen? Den if we rise up against dem likkle bomberclaath lackeys dey, dem want bring in Englishman to kill we off. I hear man say dem drop aeroplane in Anguilla, dem send troops in Guyana, seen, to fight against the roots man dem. So dat education dat dem get from de white man only educate dem to murder an to tief poor black people. Marcus Garvey say death to black an white oppressors. Seen"?

What Nose and Stabber said made sense. It seemed logical and rational to Michael, but his heart wasn't into totally believing them, although the argument was so soundly based that there was nothing he could say. He just went quiet, subdued, thinking about the course of his life.

The thoughts that now came up in Michael's mind created both ambivalence and confusion: as a Rasta youth he was committed to the truth, but the truth as told by his brethren, if taken to its most logical conclusion meant self-rejection. For, how else would he be able to survive? The truth applied to real existence enforced the necessity to act. And what was he to act on? Reject education? Reject trying to raise himself above the drudgery and meanness of this existence? No! He had to empower himself by human means out of the shackles of this terrible, conflicting, contradictory existence. He will fight if he had to, wage war against oppression and victimization, but he could not see himself like Stabber and Nose, forever protesting against the system and how things were, without rising above it. For he felt that the struggle in Britain could never really be equated to the struggle in Afrika or the Caribbean. He could never envisage the black man seizing power in this land. The struggle was really to control the land in which black man lived, Afrika and the Caribbean, and from there wage a struggle against the white man by any means. To take up any meaningful struggle here was suicide. This was his conclusion, but he couldn't find the exact words to explain it, to articulate the confusion that feasted on his mind, to tell it to them boldly and without fear.

Cherri brought the food in, chicken cooked in a gravy of tomato puree and seasoning, with large slices of onions around it, small sliced potatoes cooked with rice and curried, and greens and peas on the side. Nose pulled his nose and licked his lips when Cherri gave Michael the first plate, then brought one for him. She went back to the kitchen and returned with two more plates, for Stabber and herself. She rested her plate down and returned to the kitchen for the glasses, ice and orange juice in a glass mug that Roberta had given to Michael. They all sat down and ate, Nose eating hungrily, greedily, nosily. Michael liked to look at Cherri eat: she took small forkfuls and masticated her food finely, properly. She was never in a hurry. He used to try to imitate her, not because she had told him anything, but because he wanted to try it out. But he felt that the food would go cold and the taste of it since he was a boy, propelled him to want to eat as fast as possible. Sometimes he would put three forkfuls of food in his mouth at the same time, the taste of the food so intoxicating. Stabber ate a little slowly, but his face could not conceal the zeal with which he ate. His jowls expanded each time the food entered his mouth and his brow creased and wrinkled, his eyebrows pushing up onto his forehead. Both Stabber and Nose looked at Michael's plate, comparing how much he had received in relation to them. Michael's plate was somewhat more filled, but not that more than what they had received. The door bell rang.

Cherri was about to answer it, but Michael waved her back. He placed his plate down and went out. He returned with Ancil, one of their friends. They were still eating when Ancil entered with a worried and excited face. Cherri had developed this sense of premonition, she could sense things, pick up vibrations, read appearances, and she understood that something grave had happened. She ate as slowly as before, but now looking up at Ancil who she hardly knew.

"Hail, man", he said, wiping the sweat from his forehead. "You know wha happen today"? No answer. "My little brother Peter got killed today".

There was silence, the masticated food showing disgustingly in their open mouths. Nose was the first to start back chewing.

"Wha? What's that? Killed, by who"? Stabber said, putting the plate down.

"He was coming home from school with some of his friends dem, about four of them together, mucking about in the streets like, and this white man start cussing dem, abusing dem, because they was being loud. Then Peter, he's a little cheeky, told the guy to fuck off and the man chased them, but Peter didn't run off, and the man threw a knife an stabbed him in his heart. He died before he reached the hospital".

"Wha? Wha is dat? What de bloodclaath I man hearing! Wha"? Stabber looked incredulous. He drank the juice and left the food which was nearly finished. Nose ate the plate clean and drank his juice. Michael was eating, but desultorily, mechanically, the fork rising to his mouth, but his eyes on Ancil, while Cherri had the fork resting on the plate, her face incredulous and stupified.

"Now say dat again", Stabber said. "Your bredder get killed for cussing a white man? How old your bredder was? 13? Dat must be a mad bastard. He must be a National Front. Dem bloodclaath want make a war with black man, an dem go get it. Wha de bloodclaath I hearing"!?

"Wha de bomberclaath is this"! Nose shouted, now standing up. He took his tam off, brushed his locks with his hand and fixed his tam back on. "Dem white man gone mad! Dem declaring dem han for dis demo, dem want kill off black man . . ." Cherri got up, started picking the plates up and vanished to the kitchen. When she cleared off the remnants from the plates, she sat down and fell into reverie, as though a dream had suddenly consumed her mind, and tears involuntarily began to drip down her face. Her head now jerked down onto her chest and she was crying, sounds rising from the bottom of her belly through to her chest and escaping from her throat. The sound was moanful and pained. She hardly knew Ancil and didn't know his brother at all, yet the striking, stinging blow of youthful death had fallen upon her with such power and deadliness that she felt a youthful member of her own family had died. What compounded the death was the racist motivation. She raised her hand to her face and heard herself cry, then her body jerked softly, then slowly enveloped by a vibrating sob, it jerked and jerked, her tears falling falling . . . But something entered her mind, and a feeling of calmness took hold of her body, some spirit of peace entering her frame that the jerking gradually gave way, and the tears began to disappear. But she still felt a loss, dejection, suffering. Then she ran the tap in the sink, wet her hands and wiped her face, raised her long dress and dried the wetness, and sat back in the chair.

That night a little violence flared. Some of the youths, about six of them: Michael, Ancil, Nose, Stabber, Tubbs and Mikey went round to a pub in Harlesden where some National Front people usually drank. They waited until the pub had closed and watched the inhabitants drunkely drift down the street. There was a group of four, the oldest one, about 48, was reputed to be a racist and hater of black people. They figured that anyone he walked with had similar affiliations. They tagged them until they had passed some shops that had no lights on, and there was a small mews where no lights were ever on, then they attacked them. Stabber, Nose and Mikey drew their blades, Ancil and Tubbs wielding pieces of 2x2, and Michael with his taped pipe firmly gripped in his hand. It was a quick fight. They beat them or pulled them quickly into the mews. and started to work them over with the sticks, pipe and the reddened blades quickly going in and out, until they had all fallen to the ground. One guy fired a wild punch before he had hit the ground and it collapsed on Nose's head, and Nose grabbed his hand and sliced the knife along his knuckles like he was cutting bread. They all made noises as they fell to the ground. Then they all ran away.

The police never apprehended anybody for the death of Peter, but they made every effort to locate the brutalisers of the four white men. Exasperated, they ended up without making a successful arrest (those they arrested were eventually freed), but left in their wake a backlog of terror and fear. The news had spread very quickly about the beating and stabbing of the four white men. Parents were concerned about their kids and gave them strict warning not to dilly-dally in the street, that they should return home directly. A few even went so far as to pick their kids up from school. The police had visited the schools after the beating of the white men, originally searching for the "culprits", but they eventually gave warning to the kids that any unprovoked behaviour must be curtailed. They also told them that they should report any sign of violence, even if the violence was confined to the verbal. Some teachers pretended to be shocked by the death of Peter, and even more shocked by the obvious racial retaliation by the youths. Thus the heads of the various schools made it a duty to write letters to the black parents requesting their help in dampeneing down the possibility of further racial violence and unrest. This was a failure because only a few parents turned up.

Peter's funeral was a huge affair. The school that he attended allowed half-day off for the kids and teachers to attend. The local black community organization was also visibly vocal when one read the reports in the local paper. The nationals ran no big stories, but a one paragraph column confined to the bottom of the page. The local Baptist church that Peter's parents belonged to contacted the main Baptist church which sent a bishop to the funeral. He gave a non-emotional sermon about the innocence and soul of the young reaching God in its original state. But the local Baptist preacher, a black man, wailed about the evils of the world, about David and Goliath, and the day of retribution. The bishop didn't like this appeal to the emotional sensibility of the black flock, but he looked non-chalant and had a discreet look of sadness and bereavement, and that serious expression that characterized an official occasion. The black ladies cried, shook their bodies, hovered over the grave, and were pulled back from falling in. They cried until they were weak, all strength and resistance disappearing from their bodies. Peter's death was so savage, so brutal, that the possibility of their own sons going this way reinforced the enormity and spectacle of their emotional burden.

It was told later that Peter's mother, although an avowed Baptist, was previously a woman who engaged in a variety of financial endeavours in order to get ahead. She had taken out insurance on all the items in the house and paid a high premium, and every year she had something accidentally burnt or destroyed, wherein she would collect the insurance. She also used to throw Blues Dances where liquor was charged at an exorbitant price and a small admission fee was a prerequisite for entry. She made sufficient money from this to buy a house, furnished it in the most complete way, and had all the electronic and electrical equipment that most women yearned for. She even contributed to the buying of her husband's 18 month old Ford Granada (automatic). But upon the death of her beloved son she withdrew further and further into the bosom of the church, considering sexual intercourse to be sinful. She thus only barely managed sexual contact with her husband who was enduring, patient, and a very sympathetic man, doing everything to please his bereaved wife.

The projected National Front march did not take place as anticipated, but after six weeks, it was in the air again. Emotional proclivities to teach the white man a lesson had heightened incredibly. The youth were prepared to kill. The community leaders found this out and it alarmed them. They made representations to the police brass to prevent their officers from displaying such reckless zeal, such disregard to black people. The Superintendant understood, was in sympathy with their situation, but it would not be possible for police work not to be seen as being done. The police must be seen to be in "control", a word he used involuntarily, mechanically.

He also tried to say that criminal and Rastafarian elements were at work, on the youths and that this must be stamped out. The meeting was, of course, quite hopeless. The community leaders had to be seen as liaising with the police, as going on record as stating the problem, and that if any repercussions occurred, it could not be said that dialogue was not attempted. Some of the more moderate ones even went so far as to be seen inviting the leading police officers to the local black restaurant for a meal. Photographs were taken and published in the local press: that black-police relations were healthy and normal. The police shook hands all around and went away knowing that the leaders did not trust them an inch more, neither did they. It was purely a public relations exercise that gave lip service to normalcy.

The ILEA were closing down youth centres that had a majority of black youths in attendance. This was because they were acting on police advice: that the sound systems that the youths followed and played were responsible for the violent behaviour they expressed. As centres closed down more and more youths found themselves on the streets, frequenting amusement arcades and had more time to exercise their idleness in theft and violence. This was the line taken by the community leaders, whether they worked with the local Community Relations Office or were set up as self-help or voluntary organizations. Their words went unheeded. The only people who listened to them was a government-created agency appointed to overseer race relations, and when they did speak out and made recommendations, they were ignored and silenced. But the facade of *balance* proceeded: that if you had a black population, underprivileged and unemployed, you created an agency to deal with it. But when the agency sought realistic solutions that required some significant financial outlay, then it is ignored. *But the government must be seen as responding to the problems that existed, even if those problems continued to grow at an alarming rate*. Secretly, of course, it was rumoured by some high-ranking blacks in these government agencies, that the government continued to arm the police, gave them sweeping powers, and authorised them to harrass blacks in the communities so that they would leave the country voluntarily. Economic conditions made redress totally impossible, thus decrease the black unemployment population through migration out of Britain, Allow the National Front to grow and blacks, through terror and fear, would substantially leave the cold shores of Britain.

"This is a serious step", Tubbs was saying to Michael, "the brethren would have to watch it. De Babylon dem come out to kill. Dis demonstration is going to be one big ting, bredder. I man read bout dem dey. Dem is coward, you know, hiding behind de law or knocking a black man or a black youth when dem on dey own. So we have to play dis counter demonstration ting carefully. We cahnt attack dem National Front on we own, we go have to let dem white youth attack first, den we move in. But, Rasta, I man well know dis is going to be rassclaath fight".

"Yeh tink it worth de fight, Tubbs"? Michael was beginning to doubt himself, feeling the weight of Tubbs' reasoning.

"Rasta, lemme tell you something, if killing one National Front guy mean black man go fight back, it well worth it. Ladbroke Grove is black man stronghold an we cahnt let no National Front feel that dem could come inna we community an attack we an we go let it happen. No, Rasta, dem man have fe dead, dem have fe get beat".

The demonstration was the next day. The National Front started marching from under the flyover at Bishops Bridge Road and Harrow Road. A big fat white guy with a jacket and tie held a bull-horn in his hand, readying the marchers. The police were about three hundred strong on each side of the road, some were walking about chatting to each other, while others stood casually at attention. Those with senior posts were seen talking to the demonstrators and their men. It was already a known fact that the Special Patrol Group were grouped at different points of the march in back streets waiting in vans, there was also a special tactical number involved in the walk. As far away as Little Venice, the police had set up special points, perhaps to check people leaving the area and those coming in. At Notting Hill Gate, the corner of Ladbroke Grove and Holland Park Avenue, police were strategically placed, conducting traffic by hand. They were also on the other end of Ladbroke Grove and Harrow Road, on Chesterton Road, as far back as Latimer Road, and along Westbourne Park Road as well as Great Western Road, right up to the Harrow Road. Reporters stayed with the march, talking to the police and to the NF's leadership.

The faces of the demonstrators were serious, but it was a motley bunch. There were some dressed in suit and tie, but the majority were young kids, 14, 15, 16-19, high school drop-outs or unemployed, idle, no excitement in their lives, a hatred of blacks and Asians. They started the march off with great aggression, as though their bodies were full of power, and the hatred that they held within them now came out with vengeance upon the ground. The fat leader was pushing his chest in and out, in and out like a wrestler stalking his prey, his shoulders heaving like a bulldog's, sucking his lower lip in and biting it down with his teeth. The youths were dressed in jeans, T-shirts, some in leather, and they were all distinguished by a number of badges all over their front, even on their trousers.

On the other side of town, the counter-demonstrators had assembled under the flyover at Portobello Road. Whilst the NF had about two hundred people, the counter-demo had nearly a 1000 people. They were dressed casually, looked like mostly students, and left over radicals/hippies from the 1960s. The aggression wasn't there, although one felt that it was imminent. There were lots of white girls with babies in their arms or in push-chairs, some dogs, looking hungry and under-nourished stood smelling the earth. There was a number of inter-racial couples, the black ones dressed like their student counterparts, carried the same expressions, and looked anxious. There were banners everywhere, also badges and slogans. The slogans were unique this time, because they were chanted like a Reggae song. "The NF is a beast, an we go mash up him teeth"! Even the police were laughing. There was a guy with a bull-horn in his hand who started the chanting, without trying too desperately, the whole mob picked up the chant. It sounded like a Reggae record stuck in the groove, "The NF is a beast, an we go mash up him teeth". Up Portobello Road, between Cambridge and Oxford Gardens, about 200 black people were standing, watching the demo. They also laughed, and when the mob (as they affectionately called themselves) said "mash up him teeth", a wise guy from amongst them chanted "bruk him teeth"! The black people picked this up, chanting loudly. When the mob heard this, they changed their last lines, chanting with the blacks, "THE NF IS A BEAST AND WE GO BRUK UP HIM TEETH". The police laughed and laughed, looking at each other sheepishly. The chanting went on for about half an hour without the mob taking off.

The mob was handing out posters, selling magazines, and one or two had the daring to light up joints. Some of them were now dancing, clearly seeing themselves at a frolic, a festive occasion. They even released about thirty balloons with anti-Fascist slogans written on them. From the motorway, looking down, there was a definite carnival atmosphere, and believe it or not, an old white man, a local curio, was eating fire and spitting it out. Some of the mob walked over and surrounded him. He liked the idea, swallowing paraffin and spitting it out onto a lighted stick. The black youths were laughing, knowing that he was not doing it correctly. But the mob was not interested in the authenticity of the act, but in "atmosphere".

The NF had now reached Porchester Baths, chanting "Keep Britain White" over and over again. A couple of old white people, raised their thumbs in the air and an old man shouted "That's it, mates, that's it"! He was laughing, but the marchers were moving swiftly. "The National Front", "Keep Britain White", was written across their banner, being carried by two men, in red and blue paint on white cloth. There were numerous British flags. When the march had started the police prevented all motorists from entering any of the points they had strategically cordoned off, even pedestrians were prevented from going in. Some people genuinely lived in the area, but they were prevented from going in, and when they protested, one of the commanding police officers had to be contacted to give their permission. This took up to an hour. The chanting went on and changed to "Get The Pakis Packing" and "Blackout The Blacks", with mesmerising loudness and effort. Their strides seemed to follow the cadence of their chants.

When the NF had reached Chepstow Road, the counter-demo took off immediately at a fast walk. They went down Portobello Road, in the Notting Hill Gate direction. The police, having learnt from the riots at the Notting Hill Carnival, had already aggreed on the route to be taken with the organizers of the counter-demo, but their leaders had already prepared to carry out a civil disobedience act. When they reached Westbourne Park Road, the police expected them to carry on up Portobello Road, but they suddenly turned left. There were no police specifically placed at this spot. The commander rallied the police by radio and by contact and they moved in to divert the demonstrators. But the pace had now taken up a trot. The NF were turning right into Chepstow Road, heading for Westbourne Park Road. The commanding officers were trying to contact each other by walkie-talkie. The mob ran up Westbourne Park Road at a faster pace, and as they reached All Saints Road about two hundred black people hanging around joined the demo, the other two hundred were already linked with the mob. The police were now trying frantically to push the mob into side streets, but they would not go, and proceeded along the street. The atmosphere was now beginning to take on a feel of violence and real aggression, police running up Powis Gardens and Powis Terrace, emerging from those hidden vans that held the SPG. They came onto the main street and cordoned it off, but as they did so bands of young whites emerged from houses along the street, some from basements and from different floors. Bottles were now raining down on the police from these houses, the police broke their cordon, and the mob ran through. The police clearly didn't anticipate this, they did not expect the mob would be so sophisticated as to deliberately create contingency plans and actually execute them.

The NF marchers were directed to St. Stephen's Gardens, the police now in vast numbers, far outnumbering the racists. KEEP BRITAIN WHITE, GET THE PAKIS PACKING, BLACKOUT ALL BLACKS, were now heard in polyharmonic fashion, each small section chanting the words, running, chanting loudly, violently, as though they were now prepared to draw blood, turning left into Shrewsbury Road and onto Talbot Road. The mob had now turned into Ledbury Road, stoning and beating off the police, turned left into Talbot Road, saw the NF and screams went up: THE NATIONAL FRONT IS A BEAST, BRUK UP HIM TEETH. The various chants, hollers and noises sounded like a football ground, with rival supporters bawling for their team. When the NF heard and saw them, they ran straight across Talbot Road, through the traffic lights. The police had now regrouped and were numbering about eight hundred. They thronged the street and waited for the mob.

The leaders of the mob saw the spectacle, force, power, violence and authority of the police and made a quick decision to display their intent and purpose. The chants were now wild, the police stood with drawn truncheons, and the leaders smashed a police van, busted the petrol tank, dripping, and set it alight. It made a noisy, violent explosion. About five members of the mob now broke the windows of a parked car, jumped into it, put their weight behind it and started to push the vehicle, and as it picked up speed, the petrol tank busted, they set it alight and it raced into the police cordon, scattering them. Some of the youths saw this and did the same thing to two other cars. War had broken out along the street. The SPG/police were purple with anger, their truncheons ripping into flesh, man and woman, and they were in turn, stoned, punched, beaten, bitten, thrown to the ground, and seriously injured. When the black youths saw what had now happened, they took out their knives and cutlasses boldly and ran madly into the police. Hands raised, fell, raised, fell, and blue uniforms were all over the street, blood running like water, like there was a flood.

A woman with a baby in her arms stood in her house on Chepstow Road and looked on, and as the police withdrew in different directions, some backed into her yard and attacked her. She received several blows to the head and the baby fell to the ground. The mob saw this and attacked the police. Police vans came racing into the area only to have their windows and windscreens smashed, and molotov cocktails thrown at them. Tubbs, Mikey, Nose, Stabber, Ancil and Michael were now stabbing police, beating them with 2x2s and working them over with pieces of lead pipe. A shot was fired into the air and the Polak, a black man who always wore a crocus bag and had his hair matted, filthy, and was himself an unwashed so-called demented person, was waving the pistol in his hand. The next shot dropped a policeman from behind the wheel of a van. The brethren had now broken through the police cordon and chased the NF down Talbot Road, a young white boy about 14 was the first to be stabbed, in his back, another got stabbed in his face as he turned to look around, a middle-aged man in a suit and tie was knocked to the ground by Michael's taped pipe, and as he fell he cried and begged, but the pipe was smashing his face and body in, a paste of blood and flesh laid on the ground. The fighting raged and more police came into the area. Back at Shrewsbury Place two older brothers had spotted Sergeant Sullivan, an officer that had the cruellest reputation for his brutality to black people. He recognized one of them and tried to dodge, but somebody else had already grabbed the Polak's pistol and fired a shot, the first one missed and hit a civilian, wounding him in the arm, the second one caught Sullivan in the shoulder, as he tumbled and jerked, a piece of wood caught him in the head, felling him, he struggled to get up, slipped, rolled over and tried to crawl away, but a man known as Silence was sitting on top of him, cutting away with his knife. The guy had no emotion on his face, just a blank stare that expressed personal sufferring and pain, and just worked away silently on Sullivan. They tried to pull him away, but as he raised his hand, one of them got cut, and he continued, stabbing, cutting, slicing. Four people were now pulling him away, and he grabbed on to Sullivan's nose, placing two of his fingers inside them, and as they pulled him, his fingers expanded inside Sullivan's nose, until the skin began to rip . . .

The mob, now that they had demonstrated their zeal, was now running away. Hundreds of people started scampering away. They had made their contribution, demonstrated their anti-fascist stance, and were now flying to safety. The six youths had been now broken apart, the police were pursuing some, being beaten by people, and they in turn were hammering blows at anybody that came near them. Civilian heads were broken and laid on the ground bleeding, a black girl, studentish, was sreaming "Help me! Help me"! over her white bloodied boyfriend. A policeman hit her with his baton on the shouldelr and she fell forward to the ground. Tubbs saw this and ran over stabbing the policeman, as the civilian population now thinned out, there was now more police than demonstrators. Six policemen saw Tubbs stab their fellow officer and ran wildly into him, beating him, all with truncheons drawn, into the ground, Tubbs' arms raised in the air as he fell backwards and stabbed a policeman's leg, then kept stabbing as the blows rained on his head and body. Michael saw him and raced over, but the six were now reinforced by another six and they were all beating Tubbs, but he did not give up, and kept stabbing stabbing at the blue whirls of light that he saw through his cracked skull and blood-covered eyes and face. Michael stood up, to receive a blow from behind, he deliberately shifted in the opposite direction the blow was taking him, thus escaping another one that came in the direction he would have gone, and he turned and let all the power of his strength and resolve fall on the police, catching him in the mouth, a spurt of blood and teeth falling towards him, and he raised his hand again and silently prayed as he smashed the pipe into the policeman's temple, as he saw in a whirled dream, through some focus of his brain-eye, a group of blues running towards him. He dropped the pipe and ran like he was possessed by the devil, into the open yard behind the pub, over the five foot fence without touching it, through a backyard, then over three successive walls/fences. There was an old shack at the back of the third house, and he ran into it. It was full of cobweb, an old chest of drawers, forks, spades, shovels, rusted and rotted, like they had not been used for years. He stayed there. There was no sound of footsteps behind him. He curled up behind the chest and felt his heart pounding pounding . . . He closed his eyes and saw Tubbs covered in blood, the knife stabbing at blue, bringing blood, and they flew open, then shut again... It came to him like a meteorologically unforecasted bolt of thunder, rapidly followed by a devastating flood coming from the skies, his tears. No sob, no vocalised fears, just the tears falling falling, Tubbs covered in blood, arms raised like a triumphant God stabbing stabbing at a surrounded mass of blue . . .

Darkness came, a light moon now rose in the sky like a reflector of the world's secret lives, and he dared stirred. He came out, but could not get out the yard because the houses were joined to each other, so he jumped over the fence, walked, climbed and jumped, until he reached the last house, where he now stopped. He looked over the fence and saw two police at the traffic lights. The place was quiet and deserted except for them. Now that he was at the corner house, he walked through the front gate and crossed the street to where the church stood and walked over the foothpath which led to a beautiful playing ground under the flyover, there was even an indoor cricket pitch there, but the looming horror of the sky-high Council houses spoilt the beauty. He walked through the playing ground, onto the gravel/pitched pathway and came into Harrow Road. He walked in the direction leading to Royal Oak station which he did not enter because he saw two police there, but carried on along Porchester Road to the corner of Westbourne Grove and waited for a 27 bus. The street was active as usual, as though the demonstration and the violence did not take place. People were going to the cinemas, the restaurants were full, and Queensway looked like it had its normal proportion of shop-gazers.

When he finally reached home, Cherri was lying on the bed, her face unable to conceal the fear, worry and crying she must have been doing. Michael didn't say anything, but just sat in the armchair as though rocking himself, reflecting inwardly, and staring into space, at Cherri's direction, but not really seeing her. She repressed a compulsion to rush into his arms and ask questions, but she just lay there, prepared to take his silence in acknowledgement that he was safe. She had cooked and offered him food, but he didn't say a word. She stayed there watching him for two hours, enduring the silence and the demented stare of a troubled man, saying nothing, until finally she asked him if he was alright. He just nodded and nodded again, and told her to go. She was apprehensive and full of fear, but she got up, kissed him, talking to him and left.

Michael must have sat and slept in that position for three days. The phone rang, messages were delivered to the tenants, they knocked and knocked, but he didn't answer. The vision of Tubbs had haunted him like a perpetual and irremoveable dream . . . the sight of the bravery and madness of the brother, stabbing away at the whirled blueness, the enveloped blueness like some ancient Roman rite, collectively murdering Caesar, staining their truncheon with the blood of Caesar so that there was a collective conscience, a collective will, a collective staining experience. Or the murder of Shaka by his brohters Mbopa, Dingane and Mhlangana, stabbing him over and over as he shouted and acknowledged his death, their knives stained with his blood, spurting on their person . . . But this was Tubbs whose life could not be understood as a necessary sacrifice, but as a triumphant defense against the brutality and horror of Babylon, Tubbs whose life fell under a brutal attack as he tried to defend the rights and possible life of a people. The truncheons were their daggers, their defenders, and the uniform the legal representation of the ability to carry out murder in the name of the state, but they had carried out murder, illegal but legitimate, in the name of defense, in the name of preventing the ruin of a people, of being sent farther and father into weakness and cowardice.

The door was being turned by a key, but it could not open because it had the night lock on, and he rose and opened it, rising as from a deep frozen sleep or dream, in a world where there was no TV, no radio, no newspapers, no music, no speech, but the soft caressing comfort of sleep and dreams. Nothing distracted the course of reasoning and understanding, nothing was said to trouble the spirit, to vexation, to annoyance, but only the spirit the flesh and the powers of reasoning held him in an unending dance of memory or recall: seeing the movement/motion of time, the photographed time/space reduction to a frame, a second, and having it live, grow/expand like microscopic particles of sand, examined and understood. And the door now was pushed and a face from memory came to him, red eyes and a wrinkled face, coming out of a cold grave and coffin, to confront the life of himself in the reflection of Nose. Now he had to pull himself together, a straight feeling was coming to him, no excuses, no ducking, but a figure from a memory, a place, that was responsible for him, Tubbs, and them all, every individual one of them, was responsible in turn. And it brought gladness and a feeling of warmth back into his heart, but he only returned to the armchair and sat down in its accustomed comfort and waited.

"Bloodclaath, bwoy, you look like you been through two world wars. Wha happen to you, man? Everybody thought you was dead. Man, you look bad, Rasta! Man pass through here so much time that your door nearly bruk down. If the white youth dem wasn't here we woulda get nicked, man". "I'm hungry, Nose. I haven't eaten since the demo. What time is it, what day"? Michael rubbed his eyes, yawned, stretched, scratched, and felt hunger ravishing his insides, felt empty and weak, and a line of feeling stretching from his belly to his head.

"Today is Tuesday and the time now is ten minutes past bloodclaath six. Wha happen to the man, you mad or what? You ain eat since Saturday? Man, wha yuh was doing"?

Michael got up and began walking to the door, "I hungry, Nose, I hungry". He searched in his pocket, but realised he had no money, and asked Nose for money for the phone. He got it and walked to the hallway. He dialled, Cherri's father picked the phone up, and said Cherri wasn't in and would he like to leave a message. He asked that she be told that he called. He walked back to his room, switched on the TV and saw the news. He stretched again and yawned, then he smelt himself. Nose was watching him incredulously and walked to the kitchen. He didn't know how to cook, so he boiled three eggs, sliced tomatoes, cucumber, lettuce and salted them, toasted some brown bread and made a jug full of chocolate. He brought it in, but Michael wasn't there. He had gone to the bathroom. Nose cussed under his breath and started to eat all that he had made, and nearly drank all of the chocolate. He sat in the armchair and watched TV.

As Michael sat in the bath, sprinkling the sweet-smelling bath oils that Cherri bought, he replayed the scenario of the demo, each time seeing Tubbs go down under an umbrella of truncheons and kicks, and all he saw was the strong fat arms stabbing blindly in defense, covered in blood. But now he was no longer frightened by it. He knew Tubbs was murdered, that he died and there was no coming back for him. He was dead. There was no way that he could have escaped that vicious attack. He placed himself completely under the water, even his head going in, brought his head up and rested on his elbows. Water was a cooling thing, an element of cleansing, of baptising, of blessing, and he threw the water over his body, slowly, watching as it fell back into the bath. He rubbed his fingers into his face as though transforming the face to accept the change in his condition, in his realization of Tubbs' death and the renewal of today. He now looked forward to going back to work, but he wondered what excuse he could give Bennett. And now realised, that most of all, he wanted to go back to school. He had to wait another month before registration, but he felt excited by the thought. Yes, he felt renewed and wanted to embrace the learning, get himself preoccupied with something that would absorb his energy and time, that would suck him into its bosom and keep him permanently busy.

He did not realise it, but when he heard the knock on the door, it came to him that subconsciously it must have been going on sporadically for nearly twenty minutes. "Who is it"? he heard himself ask, and the voice came back softly, "Cherri, Michael". He was so glad, so happy to hear this voice of familiarity and warmth that he got out of the bath, opened the door and went back to sit in the tub. She came straight to him, hugged him round the shoulders and kissed his lips gently, then took the wash cloth and soaped his body. She didn't talk and he didn't talk, but just felt the vibration of togetherness and oneness flowing through them like magnetic acupuncture needles. She now poured the water over him, and when she had finished the first thing he said was, "Cherri, I'm hungry. Is Nose still inside dey"? She looked at him with a serious, mocking expression, with her blank eyes, then slapped his arm and hugged him again.

"Oh, you're terrible, Michael, terrible. You haven't called me in three days, didn't reply to none of my telephone calls, put the night lock on the door, and the first thing the man is asking for is food. Oooohhh! you are really awful"!

"Since you left me . . . Listen, please cook some food. I'm really hungry. When we eat I'll tell you the whole story. I need some clean clothes. I didn't even change my clothes, that's to tell you". She passed his towel to him and she went straight to the kitchen. While she was in the kitchen Nose came to her, and having started preparing the ingredients, she remembered that she didn't bring Michael's clothes. She ran out, picked them out, brought a dashiki she had made for him, and dashed to the bathroom.

The TV was still on when they started to eat, turned up very loud by Nose. Michael put his food down and turned down the TV. Hardly anything was said until Nose had hungrily eaten the food. Michael asked for more, even though his plate was full. "The man have a worm in him belly"! Cherri remarked and they all laughed.

"You know, they killed Tubbs", Nose started, "and . . ."

"I know. I saw him get killed beaten to death by twelve Babylon an I man couldn't do nothing about it. They attacked me too. Tubbs went to rescue a daughter with her white boyfriend on the ground bleeding. When him reached the daughter a Babylon had already knocked her to the ground, so Tubbs gave that one a stab. I was about thirty yards away. About six Babylon seen this and them ran over with them truncheons drawn, and Rasta, them beat Tubbs wid hatred, then six more joined them and, Nose, O God, them beat Tubbs wid them truncheons and feet, them feet going in him groin, face, all over. An Tubbs was still stabbing! The bredder was stabbing them bloodclaath Babylon, wid blood all over him face, an when I man made an effort, I got one lick in mi head, an I find the strength from Jah, mi a tell yo, an bring down mi piece of pipe on de likkle bloodclaath, and him drop buff! on the bloodclaath ground, den dem take off after I, but I man was gone clear. I take off through the pub gate an over three fences. Bredder, I man don't know how I get over dem walls, but I man don't even touch dem. But I just went over, then I come upon a little shack, you know dem shack people keep tools in, an I got inside it an sat down an stayed there til night, then I came home. There was police all over the place, Rasta. When I got home I just sit down on that armchair and went asleep. I feel like I had to sleep for a million years. I just get up today when you come to the door".

"Well, you miss out on some more fun, Rasta. Stabber an me was together working out dem bloodclaath National Front men dey. Stabber lick one of dem suit-an-tie one cross him face an de bloodclaath barl fe him life, like him not a racist, seen. I man chase de big fat one an two Babylon attack I, but I man chop dem bomberclaath an went after de fat bredder, but bloodclaath when I nearly reach pon him, him draw a pistol, bredder, an him fire two bloodclaath shot, but him running, so him cahnt aim, yo no see it, so I man still a-chase him. A white bredder bring him down wid a brick, I dohnt know where him get it from, an bredder, lemme tell yo, dat big fat bloodclaath pussyclaath National Front white men barl for Lord Jesus Christ mi a tell yo! Dat racist bloodclaath barl fe him life an I man chop him inna him neck like a bomberclaath pig an him blood spout out, den de white bredder hit him pon him nose wid a brick. Him nose just start to flood blood like a bloodclaath pig, an as de white bredder a beat him wid de brick, I man stab him bout eight time dey, not to kill him, but so dat him have scars, so when him live, him will always remember dat a black man give him dat. I man slice him face, his arm, him belly, mi just give him a juck inna him fat belly an de blood just run out like a drain. Den de Babylon start attack we, an I man run back inna de fight, an I see Stabber being arrested by five Babylon, but it look like him already throw away him knife, seen, but him musta get a licking when dem put him inna de van, cause him come outta jail limping an wid pain inna him back.

"Now bredder, dat wasn't all de fight, you know. Bout 300 man went up Notting Hill Station, black man, white man, an surround it, an just kept silent, an by dat time dey all kinda Amnesty International man, Civil Liberty man, community official man, lawyer man, all kinda professional man, was up dey, Rasta, even Labour MP man dem, so dem police couldn't come wid no kinda violence to we. Den dem white youth start light candle, so black man start light candle too, seen, dem pass candle out, an we just stan round de police station, Rasta, ain fraid a nothin, wid we candle in we han, an just wait, den dem black youth start sing "Get Up, Stand Up" an dem white youth start sing too, bloodclaath, Rasta, dat was someting, mi a tell yo, all dem voice dey high an loud in de police station, an dem professional man dey start feel dat dem can command de scene an want tek over but no to bloodclaath, de man dem say, let him who struggle take part, so black an white youth went inside to represent we, bout seven man altogether. Dem stay in dey for two hours an den come out wid about 13 man. Stabber was one of dem, an bloodclaath, Rasta, Stabber raise him han inna de black man salute, an de crowd a barl an love it, den dem white man follow, an even de porfessional man dem do it too – what a bloodclaath scene – all dem man dey wid dem han inna de air an de TV an radio right dey filming an recording it. Bloodclaath! dem man get clap an applause, an I dohnt know where it come from, but it look like even dem rich white people dey inna dat Notting Hill area start involving demselves – dem start bring out tea an biscuits an pass it round to everybody. Rasta, dat was a ting! I man never thought de bomberclaath day woulda come when black man an white man stan up to de police like dat. I man woulda never sight it up dat dem white people dey woulda act so inna dat kinda situation, but dem did. Dat musta frighten de Babylon dem, because dem Babylon behave cool cool. Dem didn't even have police guard we, seen. Bredder, you miss de best bomber claath scene. Den it was on TV. De BBC dem only show a small part, an dem start talk bout riot an racial conflict, but ITV showed 20 bloodclaath minutes, an after de news dem did cancel de show dem had to show an had interview wid de people dem who take part. All dem professional man dey who went to de station was on TV. Man, dem mash up de show. Dem arrested 35 people, but police get lick, 133 police get serious injuries, dem counted three dead, an five demonstrators dead to rassclaath, all on we side. But dem National Front have fe live wid dem injuries, some of dem head bruk up, dem face mash up, dem teeth fall out, dem leg bend up, dem have fe live wid dem deformity an get cripple, an see wha youth a do to dem bomberclaath. Dem man dey go take long to recover. It go teach dem a bloodclaath lesson. Leave black man alone, is we build dis bomberclaath country, we could live anywhere we want to . . . If dis bloodclaath country have economic problem is not black man dat bring it pon dem. Is we cheap labour dat build back dis country after de destruction of de worl war, an now dem is best frien wid de Italian, dat fascist nation, dem is best frien wid de Germans, dem likkle murdering bomberclaath dat kill off de Jews an hate black man, dem is best frien wid de Japanese who dem fight against, but wha, de black man who fight for England, is now dey enemy, de Russians dem who dey fight wid as bredder, dem is now dey enemy. Dem bomberclaath mad! Say wha, black man fe get out, nevah! until we ready to trod dis lan to move inna modder Afrika, yo no see it"!

"So wha happen to Tubbs body, him parents have him"?

"No, Rasta, dem still have him body inna de mortuary. Tubbs modder an fadder nearly dead when dem hear bout it. Is me an Stabber have to go up dey next day an tell dem. Bwoy, I man feel well wicked telling dem. When dem open de door, dem already heard bout de demonstration an fighting, an dem already worried bout Tubbs, not because him not come home, but because dem figure him mighta involve wid de fight. Him daughtah Levi was over wid dem since de night because she was waiting to see when Tubbs come home. Bwoy, what a ting, mi a tell yo! When Stabber an mi ring de doorbell, an dem open it, de fright pon dem face, de terror, an de tears red up dem eyes, him modder look like she was crying all night, an him fadder lose him manliness like . . . him act subdued like, like him manhood take outta him. So mi more frighten than dem, because how I gon tell dem what happen to dem son? But when dem see we don't come wid Tubbs, dem already know some-ting serious happen. It could be anything, I tink dem tink. The ole lady only say, "Come son, come in", an she just walked back to de living room. A weight fell on mi mouth. I man couldn't even say de words dem dohnt want hear. So is Stabber who bear de weight of de words. Him just say, you know him don't mince him words, him just say, "Tubbs dead. Dem police kill him". De ole lady just fell inna de chair, de ole man went over to her an hold her an lift she up and take she inside. Levi start cry, an she just start rock she body, rocking rocking like she in a hammock, her hands tied round her body like she feeling cold cold, an she just rocking an tears falling from her eyes. We just sit down an cahnt say nothin to ease de bomberclaath pain an I man feel useless, useless, lemme tell de I. Den de ole lady get up an start barl dung de house' just pure barl she a barl an I man cahnt do nothin, I cahnt say nothin, I man just say JAH! an like Levi catch sheself in time, just JAH! an she just catch sheself in time, an she stop rock, she stop hug sheself, she get up with a determination, I tell you, Rasta, an she just went inside an take care of de ole lady, an de woman calm dung. She just calm dung, an den de ole man come out an ask what him could do. I man was lost but I say him really cahnt do much now, him could go dung to de police station an get it confirmed an find out where him body dey. So him put on him hat an put him clothes on an me an Stabber take him to de police station. Dem had we waiting dey for a whole hour, saying dat de sergeant is off on business an trying dem best to delay we, but we just wait an wait, an dem see is a big man, dat him no likkle pickney, an den dem deal wid him. Dem tell him, after askin a lot of questions, where de body was, but dat him cahnt get de body until . . . all de dilly-dallying Babylon tricks. So next day mi take him by de community centre, an dem start deal wid de case, an dem get solicitor an all dat, den dem let him see de body, but I man dohnt go. I man dohnt check no dead body. De community bredders an de solicitor dem take him.

"Dem say dat dem couldn't recognize Tubbs face, dat him was mashed up, him face swollen and cut up an him head gone to one side so (demonstrating), an all de man fingers mash up an him foot, an him whole body, but him fadder recognize de ring dat dem show him dat him was wearing. Him fadder say him gave Tubbs dat ring since him was ten. So him sight it. So de solicitor an de community bredder dem say dem will sue de Babylon dem, dat even if him had a knife in him hand dat all dem man dey didn't have fe beat him like a animal, beat him like dem cahnt tame a bloodclaath animal an dem have fe kill it! See it dey, right dey! Dem cahnt control dis bredder, an dem beat him to death. Dem wickedness come out too, because dem feel dat dem was defending dem bredder National Front, dem bredder police. An dem just take dem hatred out pon Tubbs. Still, right now, right now dem a fight to get him body out of dat bloodclaath mortuary".

Michael didn't have any more questions, the world had collapsed once more before his eyes; the skies had caved in upon his skull and exploded tremorously, violently, bringing up once more the last visionary memory of Tubbs. The earth of his brain became an earth of deadness, barrenness. If music were life, then life was music, to inflame, to intoxicate, then diminish, then fade away. But memory holds the wholeness, the geographical spaces that never die, that sprawl in a vastness that would never die, never diminish through time and age. This momentary blankness of the world that drilled into his skull precipitated a temporary relief. If death is but another aspect of living, then to moan the dead is obsolete. The flesh was the tangible confirmation of life, and when it disappears, when the living matter of touch is banished back through the eternity of time, then memory becomes the sole/soul of animation. The laughter, the strength, the magnetic power, is lost to memory, inside memory, where Tubbs would now be forever. And the feeling that spurted into his lungs was one of sickness, one of faintness, of the living fact of inescapable death. And he breathed again, let life come back again, the elements possessed him again, but now he would not talk, but just looked at Nose and was unaware that water had welled up in his eyes.

Nose had finished eating and sensed the danger that the explanation had caused, and decided to leave. For Nose, *death had been made normal.* The life that he lived – the fact that he was forced to confront the possibility of physical death every day, not because he ripped off material goods for his survival, but the daily confrontations with the owners of the society in which he lived, in which he was to be a stranger, to be locked out from power and its manifestations – was death. But the power of the black soul – that unnamed thing of indescribeable spiritual grace, fortitude of spirit and historical consciousness, a determination of genetic forces travelling through millenia, that brought people through the ravages of enslavement, through the ravages of the transatlantic voyage with death burping through sea water, with death flinching between the fishes' teeth, with death dropping on salt water, flesh decomposing on salt water, and a path of bones, if traced by an underground ship, leading from the continent of mother Afrika straight to the shores of the Caribbean and the Americas, this sacred path of bones, a monument to brutality and the bestiality of man – was the dredged up power, the field of soul forces that kept him and his brethren alive, to manage life.

So with one last gesture, one last communicable touch of genetic power, he touched Michael on the arm, shook the arm, looked into his face, and said, "The man is a man, Rasta. See it? Man is a man, so expect anyting, anyting, and de frame nah get destroyed, see it, de frame is de soul, an dat nah get destroyed, because wha, it a de inna part of de I, a inna part of de man dat no bloodclaath can get at, dat is de I secret, yo see it? Dat man have fe preserve or him go mad inna dis town. Take care, Rasta. Sight up de I in de I wah". And he left with a bounce of tradition.

Cherri wanted to cry, but felt she had to repress it or Michael would weaken, that he would sink further into himself, and she held her dignity, her grace, so that he too would hold his. She went and played a record, a record that she knew he liked even though it was a couple of years old. Keith Hudson's "Flesh Of My Skin", and it came to him like a nuclear explosion, in all its devastation and transforming power, that the same thing that Nose was talking about, the same preservation, was what Hudson was now restating, like he too had had a dream, dreams that woke him up and held him and forced their articulation onto record. And that dream, those dreams were now communicating the reality of their experience, both in the consciousness of the singer/creator and in him, the listener, and it was bringing him back to realization, back to the world of lived reality, back to the wonder and madness of real-world dream that stood within him and outside his door. Hudson sang about men that he'd known who were searching for treasures in this world, of being nursed by the black breast, of the necessity for the black man to fight his revolution ("maybe today, maybe tomorrow"), and about some person/people who was/were no friend of his, the lies that he/they told, and the many hearts that he/they had broken, all now became contextualised within the broader meaning of the environment he was in, the broader political meaning of existence in relation to struggle, and he resolved that to learn ans expand his understanding, to sharpen his sensitivity, was what he needed to do. And the world had come back with completeness, with a totality of understanding, and with his hand under his chin, sitting in the armchair, he just looked at the incredibleness of this beautiful, small woman who had come into his lite like a whirled dream and had possessed him, like an angel, and taught him more about the expanse of this life.

1980

As Trevor van Zweider reclinedon the firm bed (a ploysuggested by his osteopath to relieve the sporadic but constant back pains he suffered from), he was conscious of the thoughts of his beautiful young daughter lying in bed with the young man – someone he hardly knew, but whom he was persuaded to have empathy with, and the thoughts of his own past came to him like a mystical cloud. He remembered when he had first met his young wife on the plains of a Guyanese country town, the first thing that attracted him to her was the dark thick hair pulled back in a huge bun and it also grew down the sides of her longish face, and her eyes were black like a panther, but the softness of her smile and the gentleness of her look had diminished any potential animal fierceness. It was the first time as a young man that he felt sexuality immediately well up in him, to possess and smother that soft young thing.

Now he relaxed on this bed with his young daughter in the next room with a young man he had helped, but not quite known. He had been trying to read. Each time he picked the book up, thoughts flying through his mind, the words became blurred and he was brought to awareness that he had lost the meaning of what he had read. His mind kept coming back to his wife in her youth and his daughter in the next room. He was drinking brandy with lemon and honey because he felt his throat tickle him, and instead of waiting for the onslaught of the cold, he wanted to beat it back to oblivion. He sipped and forced a kind of cough which was a kind of testing of his throat. He must have been reclining on the bed for three hours, yet time felt static, not moving. He finally got up with no real objective to his movements – and perhaps to convince himself that he was acting decently and morally – he slowly walked to the bathroom. But the sounds that he consciously wanted to hear, the very sounds that he was rationally avoiding, but emotionally anticipated, crept through the room like soft tears from a child or a cat sighing. It stopped him. He wiped his face with his open palms and continued to walk slowly to the bathroom. He heard his daughter sighing pleasureably, then the signs were overtaken by a more guttural groaning, then he kept hearing whispers, like someone sweetly talking to another. It must be the boy, he felt. He entered the bathroom and left the door open and passed his open palm over his face again. The groaning went on and on, increasing in ecstacy and cadence, like the soft murmuring of a river as it came off the rocks and settled in a pool.

He listened as he now heard the frantic grasping for release of air, the sputtering sounds of the voice as intensity of emotion climbed to the deepest reaches of the mind-brain, enveloping it, overtaking it, smothering and possessing it, and he could hear the internal clicking mechanism of the mind-brain, enveloping it, overtaking it feeling, and the voice gasping for air, reaching explosive heights and bursting. He wiped his face again, then turned the tap on and as he threw water on his face, he realised that he was sweating, and as he brought his hands up to his face he also realised that he was shaking. He washed his face over and over, wiped it, and then walked back to his room, firmly closing the door. The thoughts that now possessed his mind made him hate himself: as he tried to sleep, closing his eyes, he saw his young wife, as they locked into each other's eyes, hers black and pantherish, removing very slowly the red flowered dress over her head, the breasts firm and rounded like a julie mango, the legs slightly fatty, but thick and powerful, and the thick black hair beautifully laid out between her thighs – a magical black soft sight that enhanced and enchanted – and they slowly walking towards each other – himself a naked specimen of hard erect feeling – the branch between his legs standing out like a bull-pistle – he could also feel the waters rising to the head of it – and as they stood embracing – she holding his rod and placing it between her thighs – he realised that the face had changed slightly – that he was kissing and fondling his beautiful young daughter. The realization that it was his daughter did not diminish the impact and extent of his eroticism - she increased it, because his eyes felt weighted down by some invisible unknown force and could not be opened – and he allowed the force to keep his eyes closed – and it was not a dream but the power of real recreation and inventive imagination – and he felt the heat and softness of his daughter upon him – he was so gentle, so soft, so tender – the face dissolving into his wife, then back to his daughter, dissolving and changing – that he felt the waters of life left his body and his eyes flew open – hot, ashamed, hurt and a cruelty stabbing his now conscious mind.

In the other room Cherri was lying on top of Michael. She felt exhausted, but like the exhaustion of a little girl who had travelled all over the city, discovering the joys of new things, and the magic of the experience produced a drowsiness, a sleepiness that was sweet peaceful and heavenly. She felt precisely like that little girl, feeling her chest heaving up and down, up and down, and the wetness between her thighs reminding her of the still throbbing sensations she had just experienced as though he was still inside her. His penis was still erect, and after four years of being with each other she was amazed that Michael was still hot for her, his appetite and feeling for her had not diminished with time, but increased. She felt the power of it between her thighs and on the front of her pussy, and she felt sleepy and heavenly, being possessed by dark thick clouds . . .

Michael had spent two unswerving years of study. At the middle of 1977 he had taken five GCEs at O'level and by August he had passed them all with good grades. The following year he took two A'levels and again passed them all with good grades. Cherri had already told him to apply to university even before he had taken his exams. He knew his interest was in history, so he applied for a degree course putting the School of Oriental and Afrikan Studies (SOAS) as his number one choice. He didn't think that he had much of a chance there, because it was a very prestigious school and young people with good academic qualifications were applying from all over the world. But luckily, Cherri was the friend of an Afrikan brother who was going out with a white girl who was a student at SOAS and was carrying out a project about carnival for one of her professors - an important man who had written many books on the Jewish question in England and Europe, as well as about immigration patterns of settlement, jobs, housing, education, culture and the complexity of assimilation into the dominant culture. Now he was doing this book about carnival since the uprising that exploded in 1976 with the National Front and black youth, as well as black youth and the police. Cherri had asked for an introduction to the girl and talked to her about the possibility of her speaking to her professor. The girl was excited by the whole thing and Cherri had eventually met and charmed him. Before Michael took his exams and finally passed, he got an immediate interview. The man had asked him an abundance of questions and he felt his resentment returning to him since 1976. The man was fascinated by Michael's story about leaving home, fending for himself, studying and wanting to enter university. The interview lasted two hours! but when it was finished Michael knew that he had got a place in the university.

Now he was completing his second year and he had added anthropology even though it meant that he would graduate a year later. He didn't mind because he felt the course gave him a rounded perspective on history, rather than just have historical records, he was getting a deeper insight into the birth of cultures in the ancient world. He was learning about ancient Egypt, India, Sumer, and civilizations he knew nothing or little about. The interesting thing too, he discovered, was that there were few blacks who attended university, and those who did were primarily Afrikans, a couple of Afro-Americans and a few Caribbeans. The school was ninety-five percent white. The black students also socialised a great deal with the whites, begun to speak like them, think like them, held the same social distance, rarely entered into any kind of real dialogue or questioning, and were actually professional students. The outside community hardly touched their lives. But they were very bright academically, most of them. But they looked upon him with bewilderment, a young man with locks and a student at university; not only that, but he spoke with that give-away accent and was not ashamed of it. In fact he had very little social intercourse with the students because he felt that their concerns were not his, that the way in which they had conceived the world was not the way he had conceived it. All this had made him a loner in the first year, and he spent a great deal of time in the extensive library, and his grades were constantly good, but his ability to write was still not that good. When it came to research, he could actually read the prescribed books and get the perspective, but when it came to writing something longish, he couldn't do it and reverted to paraphrasing what he had read - i.e., he would rewrite the sentences from the books he had read and construct them sensibly into a paper. And, unbelievably, the tutor would praise his work! He felt contemptuous.

He later discovered that not everybody was taken in by his skills. There was an Afrikan girl from the Cameroun who was six or seven years older than he, and she had just joined the class having transferred from Manchester university, and she had actually walked up to him in the canteen and started talking to him and helped herself to his biscuits. He felt this sister was unusual and liked her immediately. Later, they would have telling and highly charged debates, she always winning. Her arguments and evidence were formidable. He was in the dark compared to the knowledge she had. And it was in fact she who discovered that he was copying the books he read and had taken it upon herself to teach him to write She showed him the technique of thought – that clarity of thought was the first precondition to effective writing. He was able to express himself, and she told him, showed him, how what he talked could be written down. She actually wrote down an entire paragraph of what he had verbally spoken, just to give him an idea of what she meant. And it went on like that until he had mastered the rudiments of this technique, and when he did he discovered that the thought-process precipitated much more than just the verbal. His ability to write had now begun to take on an aspect of fanaticism.

Since he had come to live here with Cherri a month ago, through her own suggestion and persuasion of Mr. Trevor (as he called her father), he had also discovered a vast number of Caribbean novelists. And Mr. Trevor had taken time out to discuss and put in perspective the whole history of Caribbean writing. He talked about the influence of the church and the bible, the influence of education expressed in the most conservative literary traditions, and its limitation by some of the early writers. He would recommend a particular novel to demonstrate a particular idea he was making. He also showed him the influence of the demand for political self-government on the attitudes of the writers in reflection. That some of the literature took on a freshness, a vigour, a spontaneity, etc. This also fascinated him and he made full use of Mr. Trevor's library. Sometimes he felt nervous and trapped in Mr. Trevor's presence, that he was suppressing an emotion of contempt? immorality? because he was concerned primarily with his daughter's happiness, and that it was not to facilitate him that he was allowed to live here, but to facilitate his daughter? Cherri had now been teaching junior primary school for almost a year since she had graduated from teacher's training college. She was lucky to get an area like Shepherd's Bush in which to start out. The classes were about 75 per cent immigrants: Morrocans, Caribbeans, Egyptians, Asians, Afrikans, etc. She enjoyed the work tremendously and liked the way in which the kids responded to her every wish: when they sang songs, she would include a traditional Caribbean folk song that she had gotten from a book and the principal actually encouraged her. She had found this necessary, but the man had thought it was exotic. The teachers in this particular school did not have such bad attitudes. In fact she discovered that children at this age were not scarred because they could not answer back . . . yet.

"What are you thinking about"? she asked him sleepily as she wiggled her body on him for comfort and still felt the stiff rod against her thighs.

"Just tinking . . ." School had now left his mind and he wanted Cherri again. He placed his now quivering rod between her thighs and she took it from him and it slipped into her easily. She felt tired, but now excited and wiggled on him, wiggled, concentrating on the head of his rod which would excite him and make him come quickly. When he had come he bawled out and she rolled off him and fell asleep, and something else now began to well up in his mind, thoughts of far gone days but which had always possessed him and gave meaning, direction and guidance to his life . . .

NYAHBINGHI

(A basement. On the walls paintings of Haile Selassi 1 in various forms: sitting on a throne with a pet lion in his hand, standing with a mountain behind him and his face that of half lion, half man, with a rifle in his hand, pistol on his waist, etc. There are also other paintings of Rastas: as a group of warriors, with the youth, with their wives, and Ethiopian biblical reproductions, crudely painted, on the walls. A Red, Gold & Green flag and banner is across the room.

The room is full of Rastas and herb is religiously smoked, all tams are off. There is a slow painful drumming and singing. Then a short black man in white robes walks to a raised platform, holding a bible, and raises his hand. The music stops.)

ABBA: I & I gather here now to give praises to the youth. I & I brethren doh believe that death is the end of life; the physical being is transplanted to the spiritual. Although man is man, and the heights of man is contained in the spirit of his flesh, when the flesh decomposes and rots away, the spirit inna the deepest most secretive parts of man liveth!

BRETHREN: THE SPIRIT LIVETH!

ABBA: RASTAFARI!

BRETHREN: PRAISE HIM!

ABBA: Rastafari sayeth "And no one knows whence I came for I have no beginning of days, nor ending of days". Rastafari liveth for Iver: the air we breathe, the food we eat, the sun that comes out of the sky, the water that rains upon us, fertilising the land to continue life, is the manifestation of the life of JAH!

BRETHREN: RASTAFARI!

ABBA: In the travellings of man there are many things that are strange and beyond the comprehension of man. But Rastafari knoweth all and dispenses his most divine wisdom to the children of Zion. The Lord Jah loveth the gates of Zion more than all the dwellings of Jacob. Psalm 87. Zion is the home of us Ethiopians, descendants of great King Solomon and the wise Queen Sheba, we of Menelik and of Tewodros, we, like the children of Haile

Selassie 1, Rastafari, we the children of Zion where we seek our repatriation and redemption. There is no redemption at the gates of the devilish Babylon. Only captives and slavery!

BRETHREN: CAPTIVES AND SLAVERY!

ABBA: Onto you O JAH I come, Heavenly father, maker of earth and mankind. Blessed is the man whose strength is in thee; in whose heart are the ways of them. Selah. I would rather be a doorkeeper in the house of Jah, Lord of Lords, King of Kings, than dwell as an I-ficial in the tents of wickedness! Jah works is mysterious to the eyes of *men*, but to the eyes of his beloved children an overstanding of clarity.

BRETHREN: SEEN!

ABBA: My Jah is a God of compassion, of graciousness, of long-suffering, and plenteous mercy and truth. The physical death of this youth TUBBS MACLEAN, at the wicked and ungodly hands of Babylon, of brutefulness, spite, hatred and wickedness, is not the termination of life. Although the children of Rastafari do not believe in duppy and ghosts, but in the triumph of the spirit of physical matter, of the triumph of good over evil, of the triumph of the longsuffering over the fleeting power of Babylon. For how long is 400 years in the presence of eternity, what is the power of ten leaves over the leaves of all the trees of the earth? For it is we speak of the children of Jah in like comparison. Babylon cometh and goeth, but . . .

BRETHREN & ABBA: RASTAFARI LIVETH FOR IVER!

ABBA: Rastafari says "But ye shall die like *men*, but we shall fall like princes". Ye are gods and children of the most High. Babylon is the *men* of this world that falleth every day, that die like *men* before us, but the children of Jah, his blessed princes rise up and do battle against inequity, evil and the machinations of *men*. For we seek salvation not in the white Christ that Michangelo painted, not in the white Christ that the Pope and the Roman church resurrected for the consumption of the public, and banished from the eyes of man the true black Christ, kept in museums for the clerics and officials of dem church – SATANISTS!

(The drumming now resumes, softly adding colour and meaning to the Abba's words.)

BRETHREN: SATANISTS & DEVIL WORSHIPPERS!

ABBA: The kingdom of Satan shall fall!

BRETHREN: SATAN KINGDOM MUST FALL, MUST FALL!

ABBA: Our God is the true black Christ, the true black King, King of Kings, Lord of Lords, the Conquering Lion of the tribe of Judah who sitteth in mount Zion and watches over his children. The mightiest lion, a powerful and just God. JAH!

BRETHREN: RASTAFARI!

ABBA: In the name of Jah they shall rejoice all day, and in thy righteousness shall they be exalted. TUBBS MACLEAN is exalted in his righteousness, all the young man of this mighty nation that had its foundation in Zion, that through captivity and slavery, through the barbarism of Sir Francis Drake and Sir Henry Morgan acting as Christian agents, so-called, of their whorish Queen, through this unrighteous reign of this present monarch, Eliizabeth I, this mighty nation of black and righteous youth hath prevailed to bring glory to Jah's children. We do not moan the physical death of TUBBS MACLEAN, but give praises to the heroic struggle and vigilance of his children who have taken arms against the evil and brutality of this shitstem and mayhem of Babylon. "For the Lord is our defence; and the Holy One of Israel is our King". No false god can take the place of the living black GOD. In my likeness, sayeth the Lord, shall I make man. I am black and comely and exalteth in the beauty of man and his woman. This day have we come to give praises to the youth of this nation. This day have we come to glory in the power of our Lord, to speak in His name, to talk to Him, not as some abstract god in the sky, that after death we fly up to meet a blond maker, but in the arms of living man,the flesh and spirit of living triumphant man who defends and gives strength to His glorious children in their struggle with the heathen, devil-worshipping Babylon who in his raging madness and blaspheme is an ignorant instrument of the devil. We do not forgive him, but work towards his demise, to his eventual destruction, for we are not Christians that turn the other cheek, that put our tails between our legs and run away to live another day. NO! We are children of RASTAFARI, who will stand up and be counted in struggle. Selassie I, Rastafari, did not run away when Mussolini and his barbarian Italian forces invaded the Ethiopia of I Father. NO! Rastafari standeth firm against the invasion and met fire with fire, death with death, bullet with bullet, and the triumph of fight and struggle is the vision of a powerful and proud Ethiopia today, that does not bow its head to the nations of the world. NAY! ITIOPIA STANDS AS A POWER OF NATIONS AMONGST NATIONS! Not through cowardice did the Ethiopian people achieve this, not through running away like many puppies, not through taking a step backwards and *failing* history, but through the confrontation of history, through accepting the power of its glorious history and stepping into the world stage of modern power, did ITIOPIA wrest back its land from the thieves and barbarians of the fascist Mussolini and the two-faced hypocrisy of the western nations. Freedom is not won through cowardice. If we were enslaved it was not through cowardice, but through the superiority of arms, through the collaboration of our Afrikan forefathers, some of them who thought that the measure of gold, silver and useless trinkets, was the measure and value of man. But the said same Afrikan now overstand the folly of his ways and is wresting his freedom from the British, Dutch, French and German slave masters. But we still see confusion on the continent of mother Afrika, we still see the measure of man as the measure of trinkets: the mercedes car, the concrete house, the buying of cheap western apparel, the rejection of the indigenous Afrikan culture for the barbarism of the west. But we here in the bosom of Babylon see a trinket as a trinket, and know its value to be wothless. It is not dream: like the man dying of thirst in the desert and sees a shadow over golden sand as a stream and dies in his delusion. We see a stream as a stream, and sand as sand. I shall say no more, but to leave you with these words: "There is no man that hath power over the spirit to retain the spirit, neither hath he power in the day of death . . ." Also, "Then I commended mirth, because a man hath no better thing under the sun, than to eat, and to drink, and to merry: for that shall abide with him of his labour the days of his life, which God giveth him under the sun".

BRETHREN: GOD GIVETH HIM UNDER THE SUN!

ABBA: SELAH. PRAISE BE HIS NAME. JAH!!

BRETHREN: RASTAFARI!! PRAISE BE HIS NAME!!!

ABBA: GIVE THANKS AND BRING FORTH THE BRETHREN OF THE HEROIC TUBBS MACLEAN.

(Stabber, Nose, Michael and Mikey are beckoned forward, and they now stand in front of ABBA at the foot of the platform. He raises the bible in the air, his fingers between the pages and begins to whisper in sounds that are not decipherable, then he talks):

ABBA: SONS OF MAN, TAKE YOUR PLACE IN THE HISTORY OF AFRIKA. THE STRUGGLE HERE IN BABYLON IS THE STRUGGLE OF THE BLACK MAN FOR FREEDOM AND DIGNITY IN THE WORLD. WE ARE NOT ISOLATED FROM THE STRUGGLE OF THE DOWNPRESSED AGAINST THE DOWNPRESSOR FOR IT IS AN INTERNATIONAL STRUGGLE. AS A SON OF THE LIVING BLACK GOD, THE LIVING BLACK LION WHO ROARS IN ITIOPIA, OUR HOMELAND, THE WOMB OF OUR MOTHER AND THE BIRTH OF CULTURE AND CIVILIZATION, I BLESS THEE THROUGH THE POWERS OF THE MOST HIGH, THE MOST DIVINE FATHER, WHO LOVETH AND CARETH FOR HIS SONS ACROSS THE WATERS. I BLESS THEE O CHILDREN OF JAH. FREEDOM AND DIGNITY, PEACE AND LOVE. PRAISE HIS NAME!

BRETHREN (With the four standing beneath ABBA who in turn touches all their heads with the bible and mumbling something):
JAH RASTAFARI! SELASSIE 1! RASTAFARI!!!